Persian P

by

Helena Celbs

&

Lucia Jones

This is a work of fiction. All characters, names, places and events are the product of the author's imagination or used fictitiously.

Cover design: Sigolene Sarkozy

Follow Lucia Jones on Facebook or Instagram to be notified when new releases are out.

Warning!

The following text contains explicit language and graphic sexual references.

TABLE OF CONTENTS

Chapter One: Punishment 5

Chapter Two: Bathing in the pond 15

Chapter Three: Jealousy...19

Chapter Four: Stars never lie..25

Chapter Five: The arrival of Madam Lofateau 31

Chapter Six: Sweet dreams in the nightmare reality 39

Chapter Seven: Stories from Europe...49

Chapter Eight: Yet another swift stroke of rod............................53

Chapter Nine: The trapped innocent..62

Chapter Ten: The American business 68

Chapter Eleven: The cruel clock..74

Chapter Twelve: The oasis...80

Chapter Thirteen: The unforgiving world 88

Chapter Fourteen: The price of curiosity......................................97

Chapter Fifteen: Time to say goodbye...105

CHAPTER ONE: PUNISHMENT

Sahra shivers as Manda's head moves slowly down her body. She presses Manda's head down and places it between her own thighs.

"Yes, like that, slowly, more slowly, ah! Don't stop! Yes! Like that!"

As Manda tries to pleasure her mistress, Sahra keeps scolding her, "You are worthless Manda, and you're a whore. But I will teach you how to behave. You should learn how to please your mistress you worthless wench."

If someone beheld this scene they would take pity on Manda for sure. A beautiful Persian girl from Kerman, with dark hair, fair skin and blue eyes. Many would dream of having such a woman as their own wife, but like often as not, life is a chance game in which some stand proud as masters, owners and lords, and others as vassals and servants. And this is her fate to lie there and go down on that much older woman. Sahra, a woman in her mid-forties, tall and with a strong build and arrogant dark eyes, and almost twenty years older than the young Manda. Sahra has but endless desires, and could entrap you in a mire impossible to extricate yourself from. She only has to come up with a caustic remark and use it as a goad to hold your feet to the fire.

As Manda pleasures her mistress who's grasped her head so firmly as if it should go away under no circumstances, she remembers the first time she had to give head to this haughty woman.

∞ ∞ ∞

A few stars still shone evanescently in the western sky, looking now as if they would disappear any moment. The mansion where Manda and the other five servants lived was a large Persian style building erected around a green courtyard and a small pond in the middle with a usually greenish water inside but still looking azure because of the reflection of the blue tiles over the water surface. The pond was filled with water only to the half of its depth. She had prepared dough out of barley flour and had brought the tub of dough to the top of tandoor when she heard Sahra ask her for help. Manda's master, Koorosh, was away for two days and now his wife, Sahra had taken over the control of the chores and the servants in their large mansion. Koorosh was a renowned businessman who traded clothing and other products in Yazd and often traveled to Tehran to bring goods imported from European countries.

Manda tried to spot where Sahra called from and realized she'd been calling from her bedroom from across the courtyard. She hurried to her mistress to know what's in store for her. To her surprise when she arrived at the bedroom's door she found her mistress looking exuberant sitting on her bed and leaning to two large backrest pillows. The cover of those pillows were made of Indian silk and they were so soft and smooth you wouldn't want to stop rubbing your skin to them once you tried. On the ceiling of the old fashioned Persian room with arched entrance and plastered walls there were intricate stucco sculptures with themes inspired by romantic Persian mythology: stories of lovers such as Khosrow and Shirin, or Leili and Majnoon, embracing each other against backgrounds of natural landscapes, rolling hills and trees with lush foliage.

In the light of the slanting beams of the setting sun the silk fabric of the lean pillows glistered almost dazzlingly, and Manda had to close her eyes with long eyelashes and blink several times before her pupils were small enough to look directly at a half-naked Sahra.

"Oh I am sorry mistress. I didn't mean to disturb. I thought I heard you call out to me..." Manda sounded embarrassed and looked to the floor.

"No you are not disturbing dear. Come on inside! Don't stay there at the threshold. Come in and slam that door shut behind yourself."

6

Manda was still hesitant. She had never seen Sahra in this condition before. She knew the other servant, Omme Salameh, helped lady Sahra with bathing, but Omme Salameh was an old woman, and who cared if a woman in her sixties would see them naked? Manda felt compelled however to raise her look to the lady of the house as she'd vividly asked of it. The glister of that with gold embroidered glamorous silk dazzled her eyes again and the haze before her eyes gave way to a sharp shapely contour of an attractive woman in her forties only slowly. Sahra was wearing those floral pattern panties his husband had imported from France latterly. And except for the light orange Kashmir blanket with the sketch of Bengal tigers covering her breasts she was naked. Manda'd seen only a black and white blurred picture of those panties in a women's fashion magazine the master had discarded in the rubbish pile in front of the mansion. These were but in a comely pink.

"Why so shy? Come inside! Don't stay there glaring at me like that."

"Lady but don't you think it's not an appropriate time for me to enter?"

"No, you mean this situation," Sahra laughed heartily, and then after a small pause and with an expression as if having just come up with a witty remark she said, "actually this suits the situation. Well you know Omme Salame is sick, so I need someone to help me bath myself."

"I saw Omme Salameh this morning and she didn't look ill at all."

"That was this morning. Come in! I won't repeat again! You don't want that I set you on the street, do you? A servant is supposed to obey!"

Still hesitant, Manda forced her foot to sit across the threshold. She entered the room and turned round to shut the door.

"Come sit beside me." Sahra lay on a low bed but pointed overbearingly with her finger towards the floor in its front for Manda to sit. Manda sat slowly beside the bed and now Sahra's knees were level to her face. Manda's build was a bit short. She stared at Sahra's body while Sahra rose to reach to touch her head. She stroked it as if caressing a child's hair. Manda didn't move.

"You know I was also young like you. Now I am old. As soon as a woman grows older than forty no one is interested in her in this land. You have beautiful eyes."

"I don't know how I can help you bathing here lady Sahra. What are we doing here?"

"You don't get it, do you? May I ask you a question? How do you find me?"

"You are a kind woman lady."

Sahra smiled at the girl's utter obedience, "No I didn't mean that. Do you like my looks? Do I look attractive to you?"

"Attractive? Yes of course you are. You are the lady of this house."

Sahra laughed at the foreseeable answer but turned it into her own advantage quick. "Come here I want to show you something," she then produced a small magazine her husband had brought from Tehran from behind the bed, which had been imported from Paris. It was an erotic journal depicting men and women doing oral sex on one another. Sahra had actually found it while secretly searching among Koorosh's materials in his work room. Having seen the nude figures for a short moment, Manda looked away but Sarah's reaction was prompt, "Don't look away. Look!" She pointed to a picture a man was doing oral on a woman. "You see, this is how it is in Europe. Ladies are held in esteem."

For some moments the room turned silent. Soon after, the fast breathing of a horny Sahra was getting more and more audible.

"I want you to do this for me!"

"But that servant is a man, not a woman."

The sound of a slap reverberated in the room. Sahra's palm landed on Manda's cheek with a blow which sounded as if a tumbler just fell and shattered into a hundred pieces.

"Don't you reply unless you are asked, you shameless beggar!"

Poor Manda looked to the floor while Sahra began playing with her own bosom. She addressed Manda shortly after:

"I need your touch on my skin! I need you to touch me!"

Manda was motionless. She was confused.

"Touch me, this is an order" Sahra's voice was with a commanding tone now. She grabbed Manda's hand and put it on her own thigh. "Caress me, slowly!" Manda set about rubbing her own hand on Sahra's skin. Soon Sahra was gasping. That feeling of being touched by such an attractive girl was so pleasant that it recalled old memories. When she was still young and adorable, and when her husband loved her body more than anything on this planet. When he touched all over her body and played with her nipples for hours before they slept together. She remembered how much she longed for the feeling of his breath on her skin, on her back, and on her breasts. When his fingers found their way down her abdomen to her underwear. And how gently he removed those panties to go for her sex, her clitoris and vulva. Remembering that touch was what aroused her more as Manda's palm was flattening on the skin of her thigh which she held up for her to touch around.

"Do you like it" Sahra's voice was low but still clear.

"I like serving you lady."

"No I didn't mean that. If you like touching me," Sahra was shaking, her voice too.

Manda couldn't figure out the situation. An attractive gasping woman lay on a pompous bed in front of her. The bed was from hickory with intricate carvings of a mermaid and several lions on the headboard, each lion carrying one shining sun on its back, that shine depicted by concentric zigzag half-circles which became larger with rising distance from the center on the back of the lion.

After a while, Manda realized that the beams of sun entering the room had given way to darkness, and now the only source of light in that chamber was a candle which burnt with a week yellowish flame. The silhouette of Sahra's naked body was cast on the opposite wall like still another piece of art. Manda's mind was in a muddle, as to what the next step was to be. She had never touched the skin of a half-naked woman like this before.

∞ ∞ ∞

Manda'd been forced to marry Gholamreza, a short sturdy man in his mid-forties, when she was only 16. Gholamreza had never had a wife before her. Because of the weird hump on his back, no girl in Kerman had even thought of becoming that chubby man's wife. But her fate was sealed. Her parents beat her every night until her will was broken and she accepted to become Gholamreza's wife with utter dislike. That was life she thought. It was the same way it'd always been. She had to surrender. The following years to come were the hardest years of her life. Gholamreza was far from a normal husband, much less kind. He beat her up whenever she didn't obey. Actually she had sought refuge in Koorosh's house in Yazd having escaped from Gholamreza's house in Kerman. So she knew she had no other way than utter obedience, or she had to go back to Kerman.

∞ ∞ ∞

The scent of roses which the man of the house had brought from Kermanshah had filled the room, and Manda's mind returned to the present to behold the long naked legs of lady Sahra. She was still rubbing the palm of her hand on Sahra's groin in a mechanical way. Of a sudden Sahra swiveled around on her hips and laid her feet on Manda's tiny shoulders and her legs bent on the two sides of Manda's head. The scene was bizarre: A rather slim 23-year-old girl sitting in front of a large bed on the floor her full body covered in a striped green and white long dress down to her toes, and a woman wearing 'only' lots

10

of jewelry and those twenties French panties, her feet on the tiny girl's shoulders. "Take them off," Sahra ordered.

Manda obeyed and pulled the panties off Sahra's shaved legs. There came out those privates. Manda was afraid. She had never done this before for a woman. "Lick it! Just play with it with your mouth and lick all over!"

A few minutes passed. Manda had neared her mouth to Sahra's vulva and had kissed once. And then again, after several moments, another time. It was weird, and it felt humiliating, very humiliating. But did she have another choice?

Soon her tongue was stroking Sahra's clit in a rhythm which had Sahra's nipples tightening and her pussy dampening. Sahra began to groan. Life was usually hard, but how beautiful it could become at moments. She remembered how the old Omme Salameh was doing the same thing before bathing her the other day. She couldn't look at that wrinkled face of that old woman any longer. She rose her head to watch that beautiful young face between her thighs again. Manda's expression was sad but her eyes looked beautiful even though closed. Her sadness turned Sahra on. She loved to watch others trouble themselves for her sake. "You must give me an orgasm." The command was clear. Manda opened her eyes to watch Sahra for a moment and saw her looking at the lash she used for punishing disobedient servants or slaves hanging from the side wall. She closed her eyes and prepared herself for the worst to come. That moment was not far. Sahra's moaning grew louder signaling Manda something was happening with her body. Soon drops appeared hanging down her snatch, "The rug is precious Chinese silk, if you ruin it with your carelessness you will have to starve as long as you pay for its cost!"

Manda wiped the drops of liquid around Sahra's slit with her fingers and continued with licking. Soon Sahra's body began to shake wildly. She pressed herself into Manda's mouth but Manda's chest heaved and her mouth parted from Sahra's body. She gushed all what she'd eaten that evening on that costly rug of Sahra's. She coughed hard for a minute but she didn't dare look up. Of course she knew the lady of the house was looking at her with fury. Several moments passed as Sahra was looking at that rug. She looked angry but in her heart she was relieved. That rug you could wash once in a hot tub for half an hour or so. But she enjoyed how Manda sat there in fear, while drops of Sahra's ejaculation trickled down her chin. "I will punish you for this!" She shouted at the woman half her age and stood up and went straight to the hanging lash. "Undress yourself!"

Manda undressed her torso as fast as she could while remaining seated. And the first stroke landed on her bare back one second later. While landing the blows, Sahra looked at that fair skin and projecting young breasts. Those breasts she loved to touch in that moment but she wasn't in a hurry. They were already hers she thought. Everything had went on according to her plan. "This girl won't spill the beans, never talk." She was so sure and happy at that moment. She thought again how beautiful life was as she landed the next stroke on Manda's bare back.

∞ ∞ ∞

"I can't sleep on my back." Manda's voice was wobbling out of pain as she lied on her front beside Omme Salameh in the servants room.

Omme Salameh touched Manda's hair with affection and whispered in the dark of the night. "Shush, my child. It is hard I know. She also did that to me many years ago, many times. I tell you this secret only because I love you so much. And I give you a piece of advice. Try to be patient my child. Don't put up resistance. She will break you in more easily than she breaks in her new shoes her husband brings her from Tehran. Just pray to God. Some day you will get used to it."

Manda broke into tears, "If God could only see how his servant suffers! Oh my why did fate bring this for me. Who did I wrong or when did I sin against God?"

"Nothing child. You have no sins other than being born as a servant. Aristocrats and the rich have always been in their place, we on the other hand have been miserable through generations. Try to submit to her without question. Don't ever think of rebelling. And then you'll see that God Almighty opens the door of fortune to you. What fortune higher than survival for us? Lady Sahra loves to be caressed with our lips. She's just a human, she's not an evil. You would want the same in her shoes."

"No, God no! She forced me to do things! I am so shameful! Why does she do that to me?! It's disgusting!" Manda tried not to sob while having owned up to the most inconvenient.

"It's not important. Listen to me carefully my child and calm down. Do that for her and she will refrain from punishing you forever! She will even surround you with her kindness. She will buy you beautiful things, and fruits."

"Fruits?! Such as onions?"

Omme Salameh laughed. "No, fruits are not onions. Onions are what they give to the poor and to their slaves. Fruits are such as apples, cherries... Or those pomegranates whose juice Master Koorosh is fond of. They are very delicious."

Manda knitted her brow, "I know what apples are. I have eaten them quite often. I just thought onions are also apples."

"Sleep my child," Omme Salameh stroked Manda's hair so long that she fell asleep. The room's window was open and the moonlight shone in. A cool breeze moved Manda's unkempt hair.

∞ ∞ ∞

The master of the house was back from his trip to Tehran and was talking to his wife in their bedroom. It sounded like they squabbled about something. Whenever Koorosh was back from business in Tehran, all the staff of the house knew there was a quarrel in store. Omme Salameh said it was because Master Koorosh had another wife in Tehran. But Soraya, another servant who was in her mid-thirties and who had recently come to Yazd from Zabol, a city 200 miles to the east, said it was only an affair. Soraya was short and fat. She had long eyebrows and very dark eyes and curly black her. Her brow was wrinkled between the eyes and thus she looked as if she frowned all the time. Most servants shunned her because they said she spied on others

13

and had a strong liking for backbiting. She had said anyone she'd seen with her own eyes how Master Koorosh had grabbed a beautiful visiting woman's hip. That woman was not Persian she'd said. She was blond and tall, and dressed like the women in those magazines Koorosh sometimes brought from Tehran, showing fashionable European women on their pages. "She was from Paris for sure," she insisted.

CHAPTER TWO: BATHING IN THE POND

Manda walked the road towards the mansion under the rays of the shining sun. The rutted dusty path snaked through the parched fields which came between the town and the mansion. She'd bought a bag full of bread from Yazd's most expensive bakery on the order of Lady Sahra for the feast of Yalda, the longest night of the year.

Lady Sahra's behavior toward Manda had changed obviously only too much since Koorosh, Sahra's husband, had arrived from Tehran. She behaved as if nothing had happened between them, as if Sahra had never whipped Manda because she hadn't been able to swallow a whole load of Sahra's bodily fluids that one night.

Sahra's dress touched the traces the lash had left on her back, and combined with the hot wind blowing on Manda's cheeks, it made her breathe with hardship as small droplets of tear appeared around her eyelids.

She had prayed the night before to God that this time Koorosh would stay longer than usual and Sahra wouldn't wreak havoc on her when he was away.

When she arrived in the mansion she saw the couple quarreling again in the middle of the courtyard, loud enough for everyone to vividly make out what they said no matter where in the mansion they were.

"You are a decrepit wraith," the man of the house roared.

Koorosh was tall and muscular, and reckless of how others felt about his rash and rude behavior. They said that he was in love with only one thing in life, money. Other things he never cared about. Money would bring joy to life, and sex. As much as Sahra was powerful against her servants, she was helpless in front of Koorosh. What could a Persian woman do when her husband ignored or abused her? Abused was maybe not the proper word, because it was actually what Sahra so much hankered after, though in its sensual sense. She wanted so much to be sexually abused by her husband. Koorosh was a few years younger, in his late thirties. He had grown a light brown narrow mustache which gave him a masculine face. The few gray wisps on his full head of hair enhanced his mature aura. Sahra found all but everything about his younger husband so much alluring, except for one thing, the most important thing, and the most painful of all. He was never interested in making love with her, let alone playing games, and that for many years now. So there was Sahra and her carnal desires and no one to gratify them except Omme Salameh. Omme Salameh!! That over sixty-year-old woman with shriveled skin and gaunt face. No wonder Sahra wanted her only to go down on her. She didn't want to see that haggard face on that long, scrawny neck that rose out of that ragged collar but only feel the touch of that warm mouth on her sex.

The only light in her life was now Manda. Oh Manda, this attractive young girl with fair skin and always blushed cheeks. Maybe Manda hated that night when she had to lick Sahra's private parts out of fear of punishment, the punishment that in the end was actually inflicted on her only because she had to vomit Sahra's vaginal fluid. Manda didn't know that Sahra's experience with her was the best thing happened to Sahra for many years. Her heart trembled as she was overwhelmed by the pleasure Manda'd given to her. Manda was the only joy Sahra had found in her miserable, monotonous life. The only reason she'd play with her privates in bed when alone late in the night while her husband was probably fingering and teasing other younger women in Tehran. Maybe even women from Europe? Manda was so shy and modest Sahra was perfectly sure she'd never divulge their common secrets to anyone. In contrast to Soraya indeed. Soraya would tell all. No, she would spread hearsays about matters which had never taken place in the first place. Sahra had thought about getting involved with Soraya in some kind of sexual relationship once or twice but each time she kept back with fear. She was even sometimes afraid of Soraya, with her ever frowning brow. Sahra could seldom remain strong enough vis-à-vis Soraya or other servants and could somehow never manage a strong front with them. The only servants she could treat high-handedly were Omme Salameh and Manda.

∞ ∞ ∞

"You are just an old woman Sahra, accept this!"

16

Koorosh's sizzling remark made Sahra react, "You are only angry because we could never have a child. But you should be angry with yourself! Because it's your fault, it's your problem! If it'd been my fault you'd have divorced me long ago! You'd have thrown me away like one of those stupid magazines you look through so intently for a while and then get bored with! Koorosh it's your fear to lose your face you can't get along with. That you're impotent!"

The sound of a harsh slap on the cheek of a woman's face rang in the mansion. Sahra broke into tears as Koorosh left the courtyard swearing, "Stupid whore! I should have killed your father right at the beginning so that you would respect me today. It's the flawed raising of your parents which made you the insolent, disobedient wife you are today. A wife must obey her husband!"

Sahra stood there rooted to the spot and heart broken. She felt so lonesome as if she stood in a huge desert with no light shining at all, no moon, no stars, and no one was around for hundreds of miles. She panted as her muted sobbing could be heard only up to the weeping willow tree.

∞ ∞ ∞

Two hours later Koorosh was still agitated because of his quarrel with his own wife. He had boxed himself in the large guests room he received other rich and famous businessmen from Yazd area or from Tehran. Two rows of armchairs with intricate Persian embroidery and pompous carvings on wood lined the two sides of the room. A French made floor standing pendulum clock decorated a corner. Beside it and at the end of the room opposite the entrance door there was a large sofa with a heading of silver with cast sculptures depicting the legendary epic Persian hero Rostam beheading the White Demon in his trip to Mazandaran. Koorosh sat on this sofa in moments like this reminiscing the past or contriving con games to swindle money from his fellow members of the business trade.

Often when agitated, he longed for sex as a soothing tranquilizer. Should he go to Sahra again and just ask for it? Never ever he thought. He didn't feel any restrain but more importantly he was not attracted to

17

this woman in the least. She was neither attractive as Omme Salameh always insisted when talking to him about how thankful he should be to have such a precious wife, neither was she good-humored. It was hot in the room. He stood up from the sofa and removed his bow tie and put it on the table which was in the middle of the room between the two rows of armchairs. He divested himself of his garments, except for his underpants, and went to the wooden window with unsmooth glass from Mashhad to watch the Moon which was framed with all its roundness in it. The Moon's surface looked even more unsmooth than usual from behind that handmade glass pane. He drew in a long breath and looked at the willow tree beside the pond in the courtyard. He remembered how his father wanted to get rid of that tree because it was the source of many bothersome mosquitoes but his mother's insistence prevented that tree from being felled by the workers he'd hired once. "We shouldn't fell the only large tree in this otherwise treeless mansion." He remembered how she loved to plant flowers and small bushes in the narrow strip of soiled ground between the courtyard's paving and the pond curb: roses, orchids, and daisies. She was a gem. He tried to spot the roses she'd planted and given to him as a gift on his tenth birthday. They were between a corner of the pond and the willow tree but he couldn't see them although it was spring and they must have been full of red blossoms. He narrowed his eyes and tried to focus on the edge of the pond through the flawed texture of the glass but he couldn't make out the roses. Instead he saw something, or someone, moving. He looked carefully. It was a woman washing her legs in the pond. The legs were naked all the way up to her groins. They were beautiful and lean. That was not a scene you could easily see in this godforsaken land. Who was she? He looked intently. Yes, she was that shy servant of his. She'd sought refuge in their house after her husband had divorced her. "Beautiful!" he whispered. He reached for his penis which had got hard just in the last few seconds, before being startled by the knock at the door.

"Who's there?" he asked.

"I am Omme Salameh my lord! I have brought the pomegranate juice you always drink at this time of the night."

18

CHAPTER THREE: JEALOUSY

The sixty-year-old woman had seen a lot in her life. She was an experienced woman, and seasoned in matters related to sex. She had gone through a lot, but it seemed life was always able to surprise her, to take her aback, again and again.

She lay on the huge couch while her hips were fixed by two strong hands. Her eyes were wide open for surprise. Her master's penis was deep inside her, throbbing, and throwing its load with each pulse. Koorosh was moaning of pleasure. Well, the old Omme Salameh was naturally not beautiful by any standard at that age but she'd been so patient all the time as Koorosh was shoving his huge penis into her that he felt like being elevated to the skies. Were those virgins in paradise so long-suffering too?

It was the first time the servant and the owner did this. Only a few minutes ago had Omme Salameh arrived with a tray carrying a jar of freshly made pomegranate juice and a tumbler full of ice cubes from the newly bought gas refrigerator Koorosh had imported from Britain, a land still farther than France. She wore a long red night gown and had bundled her grey hair with a stripe of old cloth into a bun. She had softly knocked at the door of the meeting room as she'd known Koorosh would wind up there each time after a quarrel with the lady of the house.

"Yes please," an answer came with a tone a little shakier than usual, a whiff of arousal. She opened the door immediately but was surprised to see Koorosh in underwear. At first she partly turned around, but then she decided to behave naturally. "Where should I put the pomegranate juice sir?"

Koorosh looked surprised, as if he'd been waiting for someone else. Perhaps his wife? That made sense for the underwear. "I am sorry that I've turned up here but I usually bring your favorite pomegranate juice around this time in the night."

"No, no problem at all Omme Salameh," Koorosh stammered, "Place the tray on the table." He pointed at the table in the middle of the room. Omme Salameh was not quick in responding and debated a bit before moving toward the table. Unlike always that she put the jar and the tumbler on the table and took the tray back with herself she put the tray with its load on the table and moved two steps back. "I am sorry I didn't mean to disrupt. I am sure you were awaiting lady Sahra but I've cropped up instead. It's unfortunate. I apologize."

"No I wasn't waiting for her."

For a moment, Omme Salameh looked down and her eyes met Koorosh's bulging underpants. The shape of Koorosh's penis was visible from under his underwear.

"So I will take my leave now," she said fast, "Do you need anything else sir?"

"No I don't." Koorosh's answer was curt. Omme Salameh swiveled round and walked over to the door but she was confused. She had never seen her master in this weird condition before. She worried and wanted to make sure everything was ok. Before opening the door she looked at Koorosh again and asked, "Is everything fine. May I help you in anyway?"

No answer she heard. Koorosh was looking at her with strange eyes she'd never seen before. As if he wanted to say something very important to her but he kept back. They remained flabbergasted for a few moments, looking at each other while remaining speechless. "You can tell me anything that presses your heart, master!"

Having ended this sentence, Omme Salameh was surprised at what she'd just uttered. She'd never been so open to Koorosh. Why should she ever care about Koorosh's problems? Did he have an affair with another maid and was waiting for her? With Manda maybe? Then he could have easily lied and said that he was waiting for his wife.

"Yes, I need to be satisfied! I really need it now!"

Koorosh's bold and abrasive request confused Omme Salameh even more. She was dumbfounded when Koorosh moved toward her and put his hand on the door handle to signal her that she should stay. She panted as she felt the touch of the much younger man on her dressed arm. Koorosh moved his hand from the door handle to Omme Salameh's neck and hooked his hand around it, with his other hand, he rendered her motionless. He brought his mouth near to Omme Salameh's. She almost shook as she could still see the bulge on Koorosh's underwear without directly looking at it. Koorosh kissed her lips softly and repeatedly, the kisses getting a little harder each time. Of a sudden their tongues touched, and shortly after Koorosh stuck his tongue deep in Omme Salameh's mouth, and their tongue-to-tongue contact became long and rhythmic. At one moment, he reached for and grabbed her hip and impudently, moved his fingers near her gooch. She grunted and gave vent to her excitement without knowing what painful experience was in store for her. With his other hand, Koorosh grabbed her old but still large breasts and then whispered in her ear, "Sit on the ground!"

Omme Salameh knew fast what he asked for. It would be painful. Such a large man must have a huge penis. She was afraid. "No, that's too much! It's too fast for me. Sorry master, I can't do that! If you please allow me I'll take my leave right away!"

Koorosh but tricked her, "Just a few seconds. I promise! It will be over before you can think of." He caressed her hair and kissed her lips and forehead with affection.

Omme Salameh panted, "No! I'm sorry. I can't do this! It's too lecherous!"

Koorosh hugged her tight and insisted, "My dear Omme Salameh, just a few seconds!"

Omme Salameh felt so pleased that the master showed kindness to her by hugging that she agreed on impulse to knee on the floor for a few seconds. "But only a few seconds!" She insisted looking up at Koorosh's face who gave back a soft smile. Koorosh pulled his underpants slowly off to show off his now hard and huge penis, swinging it from side to side. Omme Salameh, always sober and discrete, laughed at that sight. "Look at me when I put it in your mouth," Koorosh requested.

Omme Salameh looked up and opened her mouth as Koorosh used his hand to put his penis into her mouth while gently stroking her head with his other hand. Omme Salameh felt that young penis hardening in her mouth, she didn't want to forgo that painful pleasure. On the other hand she wanted to think that she was still in control of her own mouth, although she wasn't sure if she could ever escape Koorosh's tight grasp on her head.

The penis penetrated deeper in her mouth until it entered her throat. It was very painful and hard, and she could not breathe properly. "Lie on the couch my dear." Shortly after, Koorosh pounded that for-years-disused vulva mercilessly. He grabbed Omme Salameh's breasts to make her grunt and squeal. Soon they were hyperventilating.

∞ ∞ ∞

While walking back to the servant's bedroom, Omme Salameh could still feel the constant friction of her dress on her hardened nipples. She smacked her lips as a small girl would having had one of those Italian made lollipops. Omme Salameh didn't even know where exactly Italy was. All she knew was that Koorosh and other businessmen from Yazd imported sweets, bonbons, lollipops, dresses and fancy shoes from that land. Master Koorosh had once been in that civilized country, with all its sculptures and historical edifices and remnants from its glorious past. Koorosh was always dressed in an Italian suit when out and about. Oh, he was so dashing, intelligent and handsome! Omme Salameh's heart pounded as she thought of a man thirty years younger than her, and of the moments that handsome man had enjoyed her own throat. It'd been painful but extremely beautiful.

She entered the room and felt her way through the darkness with her feet among the wide spread mattresses of other servants. She arrived at her mattress beside Manda's and lay herself slowly so as not to wake her. She could see the crescent of the moon shining in through the old small window. She couldn't sleep out of excitement. She covered herself under the ragged cotton cover which was thread bare at several places.

She reached for her own breasts under her dress and then moved her hand to her crotch, rubbing it quickly and firmly. She was so aroused she got ignorant that her movement might wake other people lying in that room. When orgasm came waves of shudder passed through her body.

∞ ∞ ∞

The following night Omme Salameh couldn't take her eyes off the old clock hanging on the wall in the corner of the kitchen as she cut pomegranates to prepare juice for Koorosh. She was going to take him the juice at sharp eight o'clock. She thought for a moment of Sahra. What would have happened last night had she seen Omme Salameh with her husband in that situation? She would have killed them both. Was Omme Salameh playing a dangerous game? Sure enough, but her feelings led her on.

She squeezed the pomegranates carefully to extract the juice without losing the disturbing seeds into the tumbler. She then threw three tiny ice cubes in and stirred the mixture as the large clock hand approached the figure of eight in a tiny step. She hastily put the tumbler on the tray and left the kitchen to go to the meeting room which was located diagonally across the courtyard. She could see through the windows of the room that the light was on. Her heart raced with each step she took toward Koorosh's room. She remembered that strong body, and the firm grip of those young hands on the back of her head.

She opened the entrance door to the corridor leading to the meeting room and strode to knock at the door but she heard someone's voice from inside. She pricked up her ears. She heard Koorosh making joyful noises. She was petrified. She felt cold. She rushed back outside to the window to watch what was going on. Through a small crack in the thick heavy wool curtain she saw what made her all but burst into tears.

Koorosh was standing in front of the large kingly sofa, naked, and his cock erect. There was a woman with tiny build, narrow and angular, with her breasts hanging down, and on her all fours as he thrust his dick into her throat with all his force. Her head was not clearly visible. Omme Salameh was all eyes to recognize the perpetrator. It was hard as the woman was topless, wearing slacks that was part of the uniform for every servant in the mansion. She took her time till at one moment, when that long penis left that mouth for a short moment, the girl looked in the direction of the window. "You disgusting bitch you! I will cut you into pieces!" whispered Omme Salameh in rageful disbelief.

CHAPTER FOUR: STARS NEVER LIE

A chill breeze blew over Yazd. This town in the middle of a huge desert was the last place where non-Muslim minorities were still free in Persia, and the last stronghold of a shaky equilibrium amongst various ethnic groups which still let a relatively fair and tolerant attitude toward minorities such as Zoroastrians, to which the young and beautiful Manda belonged.

A thousand and three hundred years ago and over one thousand miles to the west in the mountainous region of Nahavand, the Persian Imperial Army had been decisively defeated in the battle against the invading warriors from Arabia, and after that Persian women were traded as slaves, and regarded as not more than precious booties in the war against Persian infidels. Only in secluded areas and towns were women safe, and Yazd was one of them.

Yazd was a city with a history dating back to ancient times. Irandokht, the daughter of Emperor Khosrow Parviz which was the last mighty Persian Emperor before weak kings succeeded, received this town from his father as a gift. As a female governor in the heart of Persia she practiced power over a vast region, beginning from the east of the Espahan province in its western part to the parched grounds of the hottest desert of the entire world, the Lut Desert in its east. In the north it was limited by another desert, Dashte Kavir and in the south there was no clear boundary, and many thought the area of her reign was limited in the south only to the shores of the Persian Gulf.

It is said that Irandokht loved to make the men under her reign totally submit to her, and she crushed every opposition with cruel oppression. Once a sergeant refused to decapitate the father of a family who had hidden their crops so as to evade paying taxes. The father was set free, but in order for the sergeant to become a lesson for all other officers his feet were cut off and he was hanged from a tree bleeding so long that in the end he became a hearty meal for the hungry wolves who could seldom hunt an animal in the desolate deserts of Yazd. There are other stories about which many historians have expressed doubts, as a princess from royal blood known for decency could have never done deeds those stories claim. One is that Irandokht once saw a good looking captive from Turan, a Turkmen who Persians had captivated in the famous battle of Ghara Dagh in which the Persian general Bahram led Persians to a long awaited triumph. That Turkmen's name was Tuskan.

When Irandokht saw the muscular and tall Tuskan buckled into a miserable captive and bent toward the ground by rough steel chains, she had a glister in her eyes. She stretched out her hand for the prisoner to kiss and when he did, she was aroused and ordered the guards to make him prostrate in her front and made him kiss her feet. She then took him with her to her private room in the keep where she lived in her castle in Yazd. No one knows what happened to the hapless guy for sure. One rumor says she sat on his face for him to worship her privates, but forgot that the guy had been in chains and could not signal her or do anything when he was suffocated, and she found out only too late that he didn't breathe anymore. Another rumor says the princess decided to punish the captive because he'd refused to kiss her feet for many times. She whipped him so long with a long leather lash that he, already weakened by thirst, hunger and exhaustion, collapsed to death. However, royal historians correctly point out that all these narrations are probably made up by the malevolent envious. Those descendants of vassals who bear the grudge that kings have to rule with an iron fist to make their very lives, the lives of those vassals, secure.

∞ ∞ ∞

Fate has played a lot with descendants of Adam and Eva. Life has always been a playground for the children of God. As Manda washed her up-to-her-hips bare legs in the pond she watched the reflection of her own beautiful countenance on the still surface of the water, but alas, she didn't know that she was looking at the face of Princess Irandokht, the woman who had ruled this area around one thousand and three hundred years ago. Manda was a descendant of a great King, the King of Kings of Persia, Khosrow Parviz, and her resemblance to his daughter was to such a level that King Khosrow Parviz would have rolled in his tomb had he known of it, that his scion was serving a businessman and his wife in Yazd.

26

Manda looked up to the stars and recognized the big dipper. Further to the left the Milky Way shone beautifully as if angels had spread a glistening rug for the Queen of the skies. Manda drew in a long breath and heaved a deep sigh. Persians believed sighing was good for the soul, that with letting it out you'd give vent to the amassed grief. Tears welled up in her eyes as she remembered how her mother told her stories about past Kings and how those kings consulted astrologers to know if odds were in favor of or against their triumph in a war.

Her mother used to caress her dark soft hair while telling stories. They used to lie on a simple mat made of long reeds and bundled by long old drawn-out strings of cotton. She missed those times so much. The memory of the warm loving embrace of her mother was among few things she would reminisce and bask in. How peaceful were her strokes and her whispers. "Oh mother! I miss you so much!" She said under her breath.

A piece of black cloud covered the moon of a sudden and the courtyard was swallowed by darkness. At this time, Manda saw Omme Salameh, holding a tray with a tumbler on it, walk along the diagonal of the courtyard toward the meeting room where Koorosh used to overnight whenever he'd had an altercation with his wife. "Omme Salameh! Omme Salameh!" Manda called out to Omme Salameh but in vain. Omme Salameh was so much absorbed in her own thoughts and focused on keeping going that she didn't notice Manda's calls.

But shortly after, Omme Salameh returned from the meeting room as tears had visibly misted her cheeks. What had happened to this lonely old woman who'd always lent her ear to Manda when she had to tell her about her troubles?

Manda swiftly pulled her legs out from the pond, dried them with the piece of sack she'd brought with her to use as a towel and put her black cloak on to scurry to the kitchen where she guessed Omme Salameh had gone to. However, she didn't find her there and so she turned back and went down the corridor to the servant's bedroom where she found her crouching and holding a pillow in her arms, pressing her face to the pillow and moaning. Manda wasn't still sure if Omme Salameh was crying or not. She walked over to her and asked in anguish, "Omme Salameh, what's happened?"

Omme Salameh didn't look up. Was she ashamed? What had happened to this old woman who'd always been Manda's person of trust with empathy and human warmth, things she could hardly find elsewhere? Manda squatted on the floor to be level with Omme Salameh. An old Turkmen carpet covered the floor. The mattresses of the servants were piled up directly beside where Omme Salameh crouched, and she could have leant to them had she wanted to. Except for the pile of mattresses and the old carpets the room was denuded and dismal. "Omme Salameh, talk to me! Please! What's happened?!" Manda grabbed the old woman's arm gently and stroked it several times.

The attention Manda spared to the old woman allayed her pain a little, and she finally dared raise her head. Droplets of tear shone in the light of the moon across Omme Salameh's face. She had a vacant look on her face but Manda managed to fix her with her own gaze, "Are you ok?"

"Manda, my child! I am all right!" Omme Salameh spoke in a husky falsetto. Suddenly, she burst into sobbing. The air in the room was humid and stale and the window was wide shut, but the wind hissing through the cracks of the old window was a sign of the weather outside turning inclement.

Manda drew the old woman in her embrace and held her tight as Omme Salameh shivered and shed tears "I am so lonely!" she heard Omme Salameh mutter. What had happened? Those servants were all lonesome, but what had befallen this old woman with adamantine willpower who'd always been a beacon of hope in Manda's life that she had collapsed thus?! And how could Manda solace her?

Manda remembered how a few minutes ago she'd been staring at the stars of the clear sky, and recalled a story she'd heard once from her mother as a child. It'd been a story from those long past days, when Kings and not Mullahs ruled the land. King of Kings of Persia, Kyomarth, whose nobility and virtuousness was widely known had set out for the desert of Turan in the North East to fight the infamous troops

28

of King Khaghan who'd made that region unsafe and had pillaged the villages and set fire to the farms, and had raped women and decapitated men. In the middle of the way he found out that in his capital there'd been a coup against him spearheaded by his own brother, General Mahyar. Anyone else in his place would have gone berserk and either went back to shed blood, or would succumb to the evil faith and disconsolate, unwilling to fight. But King Kyomarth believed in astrology and what the stars had to say about our fate on the Earth. So instead of lamenting his desperate situation he looked up to the sky to foresee what normal people could never. The stars talked to him but not in the way humans talk. They showed him the way, and assured him of triumph. His will propped up he reached for the hilt of his sword, pulled it out of its scabbard and raised it toward the sky. He promised to the stars that he would not let them down.

∞ ∞ ∞

Manda crooked her arm under Omme Salameh's and helped her rise to her feet. She stroked Omme Salameh's back gently while leading her outside to the courtyard. The wind was blowing harder and the willow tree blew with it, so strongly that you'd think the wind would uproot the tree soon. However, the stars were glittering on the arch of the sky as if ready to speak. "Look up Omme Salameh!" Manda's tone was cheerful and that of an enchanted woman.

"You see that constellation?! That's Draco. And that small star over there with shimmering light, that's Orion. Whenever these two, the constellation and the star, appear on two sides of the moon and all three fall in one line and you have the chance to behold, your fortune will turn for the better! Soon you will no longer feel lonely Omme Salameh!"

Omme Salameh remained silent as Manda pulled her close from the side. She put her own head on Manda's shoulder.

29

CHAPTER FIVE: THE ARRIVAL OF MADAM LOFATEAU

It had been a long trip. Sigolene scratched her forehead and shaded her eyes with her hand and looked into distance. She could see the minarets of the Jome Mosque. She narrowed her eyes to make out the details beside the huge old building which had been a vestige of Persia's glory in the past centuries. Near to the minarets she could see a cistern and old mud houses with windcatchers on their flat roofs, built to create natural cooling for the buildings. Those windcatchers, looking like towers and thus called also wind towers were made of mud as well and studded the town as far as one could see. The amazing scenery raised a sigh of relief in her. She'd completed a long journey from her hometown Paris to visit and photograph the 'jewels' of Persia, and had thus set out for the most secluded and pristine city of all, Yazd, in the middle of a hot desert. There were but a few oases around it she'd heard. On her long way to Yazd she had also visited Isfahan, the former capital of Persia, with its magnificent Naqsh-e Jahan Square and the 17th-century Shah Mosque, whose dome and minarets were covered with mosaic tiles and calligraphy. However, she was in search of something pure, something original for her photographs. She worked as the sole female writer in Le Figaro, the oldest newspaper of France and every few weeks, if she was in Paris, would write a column or two about the history of the Orient, Africa or Russia in the history page of the newspaper, including photos she would take with her Swedish Hasselblad camera box mounted on a tripod which she had to haul along, journeying from one place to another. It was a large device, together with a Victor flash lamp and its dangerous flash powder which was ready to ignite any time and a dry cell battery. Most of the time she didn't have anyone to help her and had to carry all the equipment by herself.

Sigolene was a beautiful and fashionable French woman with a pointed nose, striking green eyes and blond hair with frizzy curls on both sides of her face, and a high brow yet another indication of her high intellect. She was five and a half feet tall, and with her high-heels she looked very tall. She could speak very little Persian and some

Russian with a sweet French accent. She always tried to look attractive and well-dressed under any circumstances. No matter if dehydrated in a dry desert under the sun, or in the freezing atmosphere of Russian Urals, one would recognize that Sigolene, or Madam Lofateau, was meticulous in the way she dressed. Her hoop skirts were light and built of an osier frame and thus she didn't have to carry around a heavy load on her waist. She had a whole set of corsets in all available colors, from crimson to sable to blue, and she would look so much irresistible if she had only that crimson corset on. However, when could someone look tempting if she was riding a camel in the deserts of Arabia or Persia or a donkey on the green prairies of Georgia? Nonetheless, much more exhausting than carrying around that camera and its paraphernalia was her wooden chest filled with clothes: Night gowns, drawers, corsets, a pair of hobble skirts both in a striped white and black pattern and several bras designed by Mary Phelps Jacob, the inventor of bra herself.

What were those apparels in that God-forsaken point of the mother planet Earth good for? It was definitely not the Avenue des Champs-Élysées were she could show off her beautiful long legs wearing those knickers which ended just above her knees. Dashing men would walk past her small wooden chair at her favorite café, Fouquet's, while many tried to make eye contact with the attractive and chic lady in sable dress. Those men Madam Lofateau looked at just for a short instant but then rolled her proud eyes to assert that the young stylish woman was pretty but not easy to win.

∞ ∞ ∞

As the barely roadworthy Tin Lizzie which Madam Lofateau rode on approached the Jome Mosque a whole bunch of small kids with unclean faces and tattered clothes gathered to behold the car on which the white person was traveling. To their surprise, this time the traveler was not a man with a brimmed hat and a suit and tie as always, but a woman with a straw and ribbon hat.

"It is so hot here, Mustafa. Please drive me to the nearest hotel!" Mustafa, the driver of the Tin Lizzie with a lanky figure and ungainly long hands and thick mustache addressed his only passenger with a jesting tone, "My lady didn't Abulfazl tell you?! There are no hotels in Yazd. This is not Tehran or Isfahan. This is Yazd, fucking small!"

Abulfazl was the head of the Culture House in Isfahan who'd called a driver for Madam Lofateau and had even encouraged her idea of traveling to Yazd, "It's a beautiful place, with lots of windcatchers, and a comely mosque," he'd said.

Suddenly, a stone landed on the hood and another followed. "What are they doing?!" Madam Lofateau saw how many of those slovenly looking children held now stones in their hands.

Mustafa stepped on the gas and drove into a street to get far from the Jome Mosque. "This is not a good place for someone like you," and then with a sarcastic laugh he continued, "Welcome to the heart of Persia, Madam Lofateau!"

∞ ∞ ∞

Koorosh had left the mansion and Yazd for Tehran for two weeks now. Seldom had he been gone for so long, yet Sahra wasn't annoyed. She had ordered Manda to join her in her room and to please her in every way she felt like. Manda had massaged her back and shoulders for two whole hours and when she complained that her hands were aching of exhaustion and she just couldn't continue, Sahra had rolled in the bed to lie on her back and part her legs, she hooked her feet around Manda's neck and pulled her toward herself "Now you can take it off and eat me out so that your mouth gets busy and your hands rest." Manda's head landed between Sahra's shaved and white thighs and her tongue tapped Sahra's clit and slit. Sahra was shivering. She thought of scolding Manda as always, and calling her a worthless whore who must sooner or later land a brothel. It was so joyful to humiliate this stranger girl from Kerman. Sahra didn't have to worry about a backlash. What could Manda do? She was completely at her mercy, but before Sahra could open her mouth to revile the much younger woman she felt Manda's tongue moving past her vagina down her perineum. That aroused her so much. She panted and her heart palpitated. Manda continued to lap Sahra's gooch.

33

Like always, man is disposed to wish more, and Sahra was no exception. She wanted so badly that tongue further down around her sphincter, but shame kept her back. Very often she had thought of asking of that from Omme Salameh whenever she went down on her. But how could she put it? That would have been so much taboo, so embarrassing. On the other hand Omme Salameh was so old, and one couldn't be as candid with an old woman as with a young and helpless one such as Manda. So what about just pointing to the right place with her index finger, or separating her cheeks so as to implicitly signal what she wanted? Still she didn't dare be so impudent, even with Manda. Was this a sign of weakness or was it normal? She remembered she hadn't taken a bath for two days now. That was Persia of 1920s and you wouldn't take a shower every day but if you were rich you would take a bath twice a week, and if poor at most once a week in the public bath, unless you'd wash yourself every night in a pond like Manda. Sahra was wavering. She thought there was another way. Maybe if she scolded Manda she would feel lowlier and give that pleasure to her of her own accord. "You are terrible Manda, you will never learn how to please me. So are people from the east, from where you come from. Just dumb, just stupid!"

Whether it was coincidence, misunderstanding, or Sahra's trick, Manda's tongue tip moved along Sahra's crack. As Sahra had lost herself in passion, she didn't notice that outside people were set in commotion. All at once, she jumped with a start when someone thudded at the door. Manda was lucky that Sahra's movement didn't hurt her neck, as her head was jerked by Sahra's buttocks when the latter sat up. "Who's there?!" Sahra's voice was vacillating. "Lady could you open the door?! I have some news for you." Soraya sounded all too curious to Sahra.

"Soraya leave! I am busy reading something. I have no time for you now."

"It is very important Lady Sahra! Could you open the door?!" Soraya was ungiving as usual.

Sahra felt helpless. Again she couldn't push her stance through. Soraya vexed her each time they had a conversation but every time Sahra had to give up.

"Soraya, please leave! I don't feel well. I have a headache. I will join you later," now Sahra sounded imploring.

"Oh my Lady, is that true?! I will help you! Please open the door so that I can enter."

"Oh God!"

"Manda quick! Give my panties. Where are my panties?! No, I don't need them. Just give me my frock!" Sahra croaked at Manda low enough so that Soraya wouldn't hear.

Manda bent down on her knees to catch Sahra's dress from under the bed wondering how it had landed there. She helped her mistress with getting into her frock. Then another knock at the door. "I am coming!" said Sahra.

Observing this, Manda wondered why her lady's attitude toward another servant was so heedful, and quite the opposite of how she was treated. Without looking at Manda, Sahra stood up and went to the door to open up. Suddenly the rays of light poured in the totally dark room. Sahra had pulled the curtains to completely cover the windows. Manda remained kneeling on the ground. Sahra's dress and hair was disheveled and her large eyes showed she was taken unawares. Soraya tried to look into the room over her shoulder but Sahra fixed her gaze. "What do you want?!"

"What's happening here? Why do you look like this? What were you doing?"

"What's it to you? I asked you what do you want?" Sahra's tone and stance was uncharacteristically firm, enough to surprise and intimidate Soraya.

"My lady I am sorry I disturbed you. There is a woman calling. She is waiting at the front gate with her driver. The driver is from Isfahan, but the woman is not a Persian."

"What is she, Turkish?"

"I think Russian. She is blond."

"Stop talking nonsense. Russians are worse than Persians, they don't let a woman travel alone."

"Then I don't know."

"Oh gosh, I can't wait to see a blond woman from nearby," Sahra sounded excited. She left the doorstep past Soraya while the latter had a glance at a broken Manda. "What are you looking at?" Sahra addressed Soraya and then she turned around, "both of you, follow me!"

Soraya sped after her and Manda followed them both. They shortly entered the hallway connecting the rooms and immediately after into the courtyard. From across the pond, under the branches of the willow tree and through the already opened wooden gate the figure of an elegantly dressed woman with long leather boots and a blouse with a blue polka-dot pattern and a skirt reaching her knees appeared. "Who's that woman? Her skirt is so short!" Sahra said softly. In Persia no woman dared wearing a skirt that 'short'.

When they reached the woman accompanied by the lanky driver, Sahra immediately knew where this woman came from. France! Her dress, her looks, her ribboned hat all rang bells. They reminded her of the fashion magazines her husband brought from Tehran. "Hello, how are you?" Sahra's voice was shaking with excitement.

The woman in the polka-dot dress replied with a broken Persian, which made everyone laugh, "Hello, I am fine. How about you?"

"Are you French?!" Sahra's next question was quite foreseeable for someone who knew her.

"Yes, I am. My name is Madam Lofateau, Sigolene Lofateau. I come from Paris."

"I say welcome to you as the lady and owner of this house. We have seldom guests from progressive countries such as France here. I wish you a nice stay, Madam Lofateau. My name is Sahra Malard," Sahra's gesture and expression were witness to her fascination of the new exotic French woman. Then, in a trice, her face got stoic and cold as she turned around to address Manda, "Take the lady's luggage to our largest guest room. The one at the end of the east row, opposite my room."

Before Manda moved toward her to pick up her two large suitcases, Madam Lofateau and Manda looked at each other for a short moment. Manda looked so exhausted and dismal that Madam Lofateau's heart turned over with compassion although she didn't know this stranger girl. However, there was no place to help a servant, there would never be.

CHAPTER SIX: SWEET DREAMS IN THE NIGHTMARE REALITY

Manda had been so tired she fell asleep directly after she'd carried Madam Lofateau's luggage to her room. She hadn't even asked Madam Lofateau if she'd needed help with undressing or another affair, and Madam Lofateau had been too new to her situation in Yazd to complain about a servant's behavior.

∞ ∞ ∞

In her dreams Manda could fly in heavens. When she'd once told Omme Salameh about that, she'd scoffed at first. "I had grown wings with feathers on them, and could fly up over the clouds. On the other side of the Kavir Desert I came across the Alborz mountain range and past it over the shores of the Caspian Sea with all its lush greenery." Manda had sounded as if she'd consumed opium of best quality or been on another fine drug. "I think it is time to grow up," Omme Salameh had replied condescendingly. However, Manda hadn't given up on telling Omme Salameh about her dreams, which had found their way into her reveries as well. And now, after a long action of cunnilingus for her boss and carrying those huge, compared with her size, pieces of luggage for the newcomer, she'd fallen asleep to grow wings again. No one, not even the old and wise Omme Salameh, was on to where Manda was flying to this time. That was her only privilege, to be free when she was asleep, her only private sphere.

She had long past the desert and already flew over the Zagros Mountains in the West as she contemplated the scenery below: glens, ridges and peaks. Every now and then the mountainous landscape gave way to plains and grasslands, where cows and goats were busy grazing. Were they happy? Did they know of their fate and the anticipant eye of the rancher? Manda didn't let sad thoughts to darken her fresh mood. Instead she flew further. All at once, the outline of a splendid edifice loomed over the horizon. It looked like a huge fortress, more like a castle, with many ramparts, loggias and towers. She was fascinated at the view, and winged the air faster to reach the splendid complex. She

39

landed on the footbridge built on a moat, though she could have flied directly into the castle and landed on the bailey inside. She'd decided to stick to the principles of etiquette and wait in front of the castle's gate to receive permission for entrance. So was the Persian servant of royal blood, discreet and judicious in her conduct and speech even when dreaming. Maybe because she didn't know that she was floating in an unreal world.

She stood tall in front of the gate. The castle's walls were taller than Yazd's tallest cedar trees. And more amazing were the trees inside the castle's bailey which towered over the castle's ramparts as though there to prove that nature always gets the better of manmade. She couldn't tell what those trees were. She couldn't even distinguish how the leaves looked like, were they needlelike or normal? A fresh breeze stroked her cold nipped cheeks as she heard the muted sound of someone humming inside the walls of the grand structure.

"Hey, anyone there?! Would you open the gate? Please! It's cold here. I seek shelter." Manda's voice was shy.

No answer did come. But the humming sound became louder and now Manda could recognize that it was that of a woman. Suddenly the wind blew harder and the trees began to vacillate with its whimsical direction. It swirled round her. A loud female voice came out of the steel grate of the closed gate, behind which another large wooden double door concealed the view "Even castles begin to tremble and totter when the wind is strong enough."

In a moment, the grated gate was drawn up and the double door opened so that Manda could see the corridor built by tall trees on two sides, and a woman whose mussed-up long hair hanging in her behind blew in the wind. She could not recognize the woman's features, but she was taller than her and a gilded crown shone on her head. She had a peculiar make-up, with two dark brown thick lines extending from the outer side of each eye all the way into her hair, so to make it difficult to see where the eyes ended at first sight.

"Hey, you, woman with fluttering hair, what do you want here? What land do you come from?" the stranger said with a hollow voice.

40

Manda realized she had also a long waving hair tossed by the wind. She felt a chill crawl down her spine, but she quickly mustered her courage and moved toward the stranger while answering the just posed question. "My name is Manda, and I am Persian. I was born in Kerman to poor parents. I have flown here in search of exhilarating dreams."

"Exhilarating dreams? What do you mean Manda? And if you are Persian, why is your accent so strange?"

Manda didn't know what the woman meant by her last remark as she didn't find the stranger's accent unfamiliar, so she should have held the same opinion about her own. She froze as soon as she was near enough the woman to clearly see her face..."

∞ ∞ ∞

Rays of light filled the servants' bedroom. Manda opened her eyes to see the small window passing the daylight, the very same window which greeted her every morning when she woke up. She moved up on the mattress to lean against the wall and waited till the sunshine dissolved her numbness. This was her same ritual every morning. The tip of the willow tree was visible from inside the room where she watched. "Hello willow tree!" Manda treated trees and plants as if they had souls and understood what she had to say to them. She unintentionally licked her lips. It tasted of Sahra's privates. She didn't like it but had got used to it and knew that she had to come to terms with the situation. It was much better than landing on streets and becoming game for teenagers who were in fact more brutes, to be smacked and raped. So she had to put up with it. She remembered how her mother told her many times that if one remained patient and showed perseverance God would finally turn her problems into fortune. Being philosophical about life and calmly accepting its facts spared one from much misfortune she'd admonished.

Manda looked around in the empty room. No one was there, not even Soraya who tended to oversleep the morning often as not, regardless of how often the lady of the house rebuked her for that. The pile of mattresses in the corner of the room ignited Manda's imagination. Didn't it look similar to the huge mountain she'd just flown over in her sleep to

41

reach that magnificent castle? She had abruptly a chilling feeling. She thought she had heard something. She listened carefully. Was that an illusion? The voice she'd heard in her dream, the woman she'd spoken to in that castle, Manda could hear her calling. Her heart beat fast not out of excitement, but of fear. The voice called, "Manda! Manda! Where are you?!" slowly and with a kind tone.

Manda got on all fours to see the concealed area behind the pile of the bed things, where she suspected the voice had come from. There she saw a bunch of roses, almost a whole bouquet, with a packet in front of it. She moved closer to read the script on the packet, still on all fours. She could hardly make out the script, as she had attended school only two years as a child, and it'd been long ago. She'd learnt only a smattering of the Persian alphabet and some basic words, some numbers and very simple math. She went all out to read that small piece of text. "Mmmm..." She knew it was beginning with M. The Persian letter looked like a circle in possession of a tail jutting out of it from the side. But what was the next alphabet there, a vertical line fixed to the M's tail? She remembered how Omme Sekineh, their neighbor when she was a child once read a book to her, a story book, and she explained that this long linelike letter resembles its own pronunciation, that it was long and was also pronounced at length. "A, it should be A," she murmured.

"So Maaaa...nnn..., Manda, it's Manda!!" and then she could immediately read the other word above it "For Manda," she shouted.

She got hold of the packet. It felt soft. She tore the wrapping off but only a part came off, the paper was tough and didn't rend easily. A mauve fabric peeked out. Was this a present for her? She had never got any present in her entire life, except once from her mother. From who could it be? Manda could only think of Omme Salameh. She tore off the whole wrapping and took the fabric out in haste. It was a beautiful mauve dress with gold strings and meticulously sewed embroidery. It looked like one of those dresses she'd enviously watched in those French magazines on French women. Waves of exhilaration passed through her. The kind of feeling she had at that moment was tantamount to when a woman from a well-to-do family would receive a villa as a present from her lover or suitor. She took off her ragged dress which now looked similar to those potato sacks she used to dry herself with after washing up and put on the new dress. She left the bedroom and strode to the servants' living room to watch herself in the mirrored wardrobe there. The mirror was stained and skewed at many points, yet it couldn't conceal the shining beauty of the owner of the brand new mauve dress. Manda laughed from the depth of her heart, she hadn't for a long time.

∞ ∞ ∞

Sahra looked at the door again and then swiftly rolled her eyes to see the time on the pendulum clock. She had repeated the same sequence of actions a thousand times since that morning. She waited for her guest, Madam Lofateau to wake up finally, but it seemed the attractive woman had disappeared somewhere in the queen bed of the guest room where she'd sunk to sleep the night before. She looked at the clock again.

Sahra was among few women in her time who were not illiterate. As the activities of a woman were much more limited than those of a man, she had gone through a metamorphosis from someone oblivious of books and literature to a bibliophile, as there weren't many other alternatives to spend her time at home. She had also learnt the language of the culture and science of that era on her own: French. She could not speak it very well although she had attended a French school in her childhood in Tehran, but as an adult woman without a child she'd found abundant time to learn reading in French.

She had recently even read a book about clocks, and about their inventor Christiaan Huygens. She enjoyed the inventions arriving from Europe so much. They all looked delicate and luxurious to her. But now one of their women was in her own house! And she could not wait to get to know her.

Sahra was a learned woman, and the Persian women around had nothing to relate other than trifling matters such as how did their cooking *Ashe Shole Ghalamkar*, a sort of Persian soup, went amiss or what the Mullah had to preach at mosque the previous Friday. She had been a few times at the mosque, and she was shocked how the senile Mullah there ogled at women. Several times had he praised the tradition of pleasure marriage, or Sigheh, what she hated. Sigheh was a kind of marriage in Shia Islam in which a man could marry a woman for as short a time as a few days. She never forgot how he looked at her amorously as he preached about the many advantages such marriages offered to society. Then he went on that if a woman didn't give in to her man's desires, the man could punish the disobedient spouse in a way he'd like, such as lashing. That Mullah conspicuously reached for his own genitalia several times while lecturing. She wanted to escape him and that mosque in that moment. That was her last religious sermon she ever attended. However, she had picked up the idea of lashing her servants from then, and now poor Manda had to pay for the Mullah's sexist blather. Sarah, however much hated what that mad Mullah prattled, had no restraint from inflicting that same pain she was so afraid of on someone else whosoever. So are the children of Adam and Eve, they are ignorant of others' agony as long as it's not theirs.

∞ ∞ ∞

Sahra looked at the pendulum clock again. It was almost 11 o'clock. "When do French people get out of bed?" She wondered. In a trice she heard how Omme Salameh talked to a woman as their voice was nearing. The faint chatter became louder as the longer hand of the clock leaped one tiny step forward to point to sharp eleven. Omme Salameh ushered the fair looking European lady to the dining room as it'd been ordered by lady Sahra, and she did her best to be polite and prudent. "Please enter my lady," she addressed the young and comely woman who still carried her straw hat but now wore a long cream skirt with large blue dots. Madam Lofateau entered the dining room while Sahra was jubilant to see the long awaited exotic French guest at last. She stood up quick to greet her, "Welcome Madam Lofateau. I have been expecting for two hours now. I hope you were able to sleep through the night."

Madam Lofateau was a bit surprised at the exaggeratedly energetic reception of a hostess she'd met only once in her life, more by the strange accent and the weird combination of French words and phrases in Sahra's speech, but she was experienced enough in stumbling across different cultures and exorbitant people so as not to be dumbfounded in such a situation. Actually, it would have been much more confounding if she'd met a Persian woman in a rather small town in the middle of a

44

huge desert with fluent French accent and a bearing conforming to that of the western world. Madam Lofateau smiled at the oriental woman who was dressed like a European lady and as to her features, she could almost pass as a European too, maybe even French, but certainly an Italian or Spaniard. "Thank you for the nice reception, sorry I have forgotten your name. Please forgive me, I felt weary yesterday when you introduced yourself..."

"My name is Madam Malard, Sahra Malard. Please take a seat, I have prepared a breakfast for you." Sahra pointed to a chair opposite her on the other side of an about five feet long rectangular table. Madam Lofateau looked at the abundant table Sahra had had fixed for her. There were so many utensils, bowls and small plates that you'd think the board was meant for a feast. There were everything you could hardly imagine were available in a desert town: Fresh stag meat from Isfahan, sturgeon from Mazandaran on the shores of the Caspian Sea, venison, goat milk, freshly baked flatbread, sour cherry jam, honey and other things. Madam Lofateau sat where Sahra had pointed to and carefully observed the room with curiosity. The dining room of this house was nothing short than one of an ostentatious villa she was in possession of near Bordeaux in France. She was from a wealthy family but the fact that she was financially comfortable had never prevented her from being hardworking to achieve her career goals in life.

They were sitting in a big rectangular room whose walls and niches were frescoed. On the walls she could see precious cream lampasso silk woven with garland. There were pastel paintings whose creators Madam Lofateau didn't know, but were drawn in European style. She saw putti and cupids on those paintings, all scenes so familiar to her. At first glance it was interesting, but after a second thought somehow disappointing. Was she there to watch the so often seen European art? Where were all those famous Qajar paintings of Persian epics and love stories?!

On one side of the room there was a carved ivory chest of drawers standing under an eighteenth century style mirror, beside it a kneeler enriched with carved tortoiseshell, both were apparently Italian artworks. On a corner she saw a wooden veneered strongbox decorated with bronze details. The precious furniture bore out her assumption occurred to her seeing the mansion the first time: the owners must have been affluent.

"I am so happy that you have found your way to the small town of Yazd all the way from Paris. Please help yourself Madam." Madam Lofateau snapped out of her investigation with the hostess offering to start eating.

"I would savor a cup of coffee. Do you have coffee here?"

Sahra clapped her hands once as if she'd been aware of Madam Lofateau's desire all along. She then called out to Omme Salameh who had been waiting outside the doorstep to offer help in case it was needed. "Omme Salameh, pour the lady a cup of coffee!" Madam Lofateau was amazed how the tone of the kind hostess turned hard quick on the housemaid who was anyway at her beck and call. Omme Salameh entered the room swiftly and poured the French lady whose fragrance had filled the room some coffee. "Your perfume is very pleasant." Omme Salameh complimented the guest lady with a big smile. "Thank you, that's very kind of you!" Madam Lofateau answered with kindness in broken Persian as the compliment had been paid in Persian. A nervous house lady cut in and harrumphed as she didn't want anyone to disturb the mood of her precious guest. Omme Salameh caught Sahra's drift and after having filled the small cup which was inlaid with gilded streaks, scurried out of the room to wait at the threshold again.

"You don't have to be so strict to your servant. I found the compliment heart-warming." Madam Lofateau had understood the cause of Sahra suddenly coughing.

"No you don't know Persian servants. As soon as you get soft on them they'll turn cheeky in a way you'll regret having been kind even for a second," as soon as Sahra was over she realized she'd begun the conversation with unpleasant words. Her plan to impress Madam Lofateau had gone awry.

"Is it possible that we switch to Persian? I can't understand well what you speak in my language. You have a very peculiar accent." Madam

46

Lofateau gave a subtle mocking smile. Sometimes minute aggressions suffice to ruin someone's day. Sahra was no exception. And then, to make it worse, Madam Lofateau added, "Where is your other servant? That pretty girl that carried yesterday my suitcases to my room?"

It was just a normal question. How could Madam Lofateau know how sensitive Sahra was about that another servant? Madam Lofateau was straight with a lack of interest for a girl or woman of any age or appearance. "Why do you want to know?" Sahra stammered.

"Nothing, just curious. She looks different from other people around. Everyone here has dark eyes. She got blue. Oh, she is so pretty you would never think she is a servant but rather a noblewoman or something, of course, regardless of her shabby dress."

Sahra was speechless. Manda was as important to her as a husband to a newly married bride. No, Sahra was utterly mad for her. Manda was the only glow in her wretched life. A convulsive rage came over her.

CHAPTER SEVEN: STORIES FROM EUROPE

"She's magnificent Manda! You can learn a lot from her."

Manda listened to her mistress as she slowly rubbed the sponge soaked in soapy water on Sahra's back. "Do you like her?"

"Yes I do. You will also like her if you talk to her."

Sahra's tone was strange as if it contradicted her real feelings. Her tone was hollow with an air of lethargy, somehow unknown to Manda thus far.

Sahra's behavior toward Manda had softened a lot recently, especially after Madam Lofateau had arrived, but not exactly at that time, yet her arrival had intensified the change for the better. That goaded Manda to ask her something that weighed on her heart. She wanted to know who had gifted her that beautiful mauve dress that morning in the bedroom. Several times she'd be on the verge of asking, only to bite the words back. She feared Sahra would take away the dress from her in case she hadn't been the presenter. "Please scratch a bit my back in the middle, would you?"

Manda scraped Sahra's back along her backbone. Sahra puffed and hummed with exhilaration. She turned her head around and showed Manda a flash of brightness, "It feels so good Manda. When you are around I am always in high spirits." She pulled the much younger woman in her arms. Manda obeyed the path Sahra had decided for her and landed in the arms of her naked boss. "I love you Manda! I have always loved you, from the moment I saw you. From that night you sought shelter in our mansion!" Manda couldn't believe her ears hearing those flattering words, but she was not impressed.

Sahra neared her lips to Manda's. She gazed into her eyes like she'd never done before. Manda was afraid. She had never seen her mistress in that temper before, nor was she prepared for that level of emotional interaction with a woman she didn't love, and was rather afraid of. She hadn't forgotten those painful lashes this very same woman had inflicted on her only a few days before. She never would. Sahra kissed her without permission as usual. How hard was for Manda to answer those passionate kisses with kisses. Sahra thrust her tongue into Manda's, panting out of the fire in her heart. Instead of kissing back, Manda took the easy way out of that precarious situation, easy only for her. She slipped into the bath pond in front of which Sahra had spread her legs apart. She kissed Sahra's feet and slowly sucked on each of her toes. Sahra was elated to such a level that she had almost an orgasm for the sole fact of her feet being kissed and caressed as such. She parted her legs and pointed to her own crotch for Manda to lick. Manda gazed in her mistress's eyes, and gently licked her clit several times as Sahra moaned. Emotions had got the better of Sahra. She shuddered. Even once, she hugged herself tightly and rubbed her arms with her hands as if chilly. Manda had safely entered the to-her-beknown ritual of giving head to Sahra. "I love you Manda, I have only you in my miserable life."

Manda raised her head to meet Sahra's passionate eyes and then closed them again and continued with giving her the pleasure she needed. In her heart, she took pity on her boss, who was having one orgasm after another.

When they both had a break, between the orgasms, Sahra enthusiastically related the stories from Europe Madam Lofateau had shared with her, in a way as though she'd been there herself. About Paris and its streets and alleys lined with cafés and trees: oaks, pines and beeches, its historical monuments, the Louvre Museum where you could see valuable archaeological artifacts, and so on. Manda didn't listen, but daydreamed about what she'd dreamt the night before.

When Manda gave her mistress pleasure, for a moment Sahra looked at her closed eyes. Her eyelashes were so long, and her eyes were among the most beautiful things even when shut. "She's mine," she said to herself and curled her legs around Manda's neck to push her mouth to her own privates. Manda's tongue wiggled in her vulva and aroused her. That prompted her to grasp Manda's both hands and put them on her own hard nipples. "Rub them!"

Manda began playing with Sahra's nipples while still eating her pussy. After a few moments, she raised her head and eyed Sahra's eyes, in return Sahra said something which knocked her socks off, "I wish there came a day that I were the only thing you would think about, that all your dreams would center on me." Was this woman up to stealing Manda of her last possession? Of her dreams? A cold ran up and down her backbone. Her dreams would always remain hers, she was certain. "You do love me, don't you Manda? I've always been so kind to you. I saved you from the street. If I hadn't helped you only Lord knows what would have happened to you. Everything you have is thanks to me."

Kind?! Was this woman serious? Had she already forgotten about the lashes the previous week, whose traces are clearly visible on Manda's fair and otherwise smooth skin?! How selfish could someone be? Is there any limit to man's self-obsession? Manda didn't answer. "I am asking you Manda. Do you love me? Or at least are you thankful to me?"

Manda couldn't help but stop licking and heave a deep sigh. The lash strokes had left their trace not only on her appearance, but also on her soul. She didn't dare speak. She looked at Sahra with eyes brimming with sadness. Would Sahra see the truth in her eyes? "Oh Manda! You don't have to speak. I knew that you love me. Your eyes betray that."

Manda was overwhelmed by grief. Her shoulders slumped. How could her boss be so dumb? "I am thinking of something for you Manda. You know for me you are like a precious gem, like a valueless diamond. I don't want others to see you. It makes me angry. You know the mansion has a large basement adjoining the cistern on the back part, beside the back door. What do you think? We can arrange a pretty lodging there for you. You don't have to work any longer. You will stay put there, waiting for me."

"That basement doesn't have any windows! I'll need the sun!"

"No it doesn't. But you don't need the sun! If you really love me, you don't need any warmth except that from me."

What was this woman talking about?! She hadn't hugged Manda even once since Manda could remember. What warmth was she pertaining to?!

"No Sahra, I am sorry! This is too much. I want to be free. You can't treat me like a prisoner!" Manda remained resilient. She was not going to give up on her freedom easily. This time she took the risk.

CHAPTER EIGHT: YET ANOTHER SWIFT STROKE OF ROD

"Ok, all right," Sahra answered. "I respect your point. You don't want to be totally mine, to be under my sway. I understand you through and through. I won't hound you to something you don't like. You know that I love you. I will fight down my urge for you... And I don't feel aggrieved, believe me!"

Manda felt relieved and even proud for the first time in a long time. Yes, that was the key to freedom, to remain resilient in face of suppression!

∞ ∞ ∞

Sahra was looking over the pages of a book in the dining room. She was looking at illustrations by the French author Marquis de Sade, a scandalous libertarian. His kinky paintings sketched women flogged, hanged by their feet from a ceiling or strapped to a large wheel, all for sexual gratification. At first she had found the figures odd, but each time she looked at the book yet another time, she liked the idea more. In her imagination she flogged Manda, who begged her for mercy. How alluring that thought was. She reached for her own vulva and touched it for a few seconds. She rubbed it slowly through the multiple layers of clothing. She enjoyed her visions centering on Manda. Her blue eyes shining under her dark eyebrows flashed in front of Sahra's eyes. "I love you Manda. I will make you mine, finally. Your tongue will taste every corner of my body and you will enjoy it. You'll kiss me all over." She just had another bizarre idea, "Could she clean my whole body with her tongue, beginning with my feet? Ideally after I haven't bathed for a few days? Then she won't miss my natural taste."

Her wants knew no limits.

∞ ∞ ∞

Manda was washing Sahra's underwear in the stream babbling behind the mansion.

That stream stemmed from a qanat, which is a gently sloping underground channel to transport water from an aquifer to the surface for irrigation and drinking. This was an ancient system of water supply from a deep well that made use of a series of vertical access shafts. Qanats still create a reliable supply of water in hot, arid climates.

The scenery was fascinating, rolling dunes as far as eye could see. How far would that reach? Was there any end to that parched desert? Sure there was. At some points mountains would appear, and a large river would flow, into which this narrow stream fed.

Manda used ash and a particular soil for wash-up. Something like chemical liquids for washing laundry wasn't known to people in Yazd. She looked at the pile of bras and panties owned by her mistress. She didn't have any such clothes. Those were relatively new European inventions who few Persian women had access to, especially in smaller towns such as Yazd. She took the next panties and looked at its blots and smears. "How does she make them like this? So dirty!" She soaked the white panty in water and covered it with ash, and then tried to scrape away the smudge with her fingernails. Meanwhile she lost herself in her reveries, before Soraya's voice startled her, "You love it, huh? Touching her things."

"What do you want here? I am washing Mrs. Sahra's clothes."

"You call these clothes?!" Soraya scoffed.

"They are. Now go away! Let me work through my chores!"

"You know Manda, why don't you just clean them with your mouth? It will be much faster."

"What you say is disgusting. Go away, leave me in peace."

But Soraya was not going to let loose. She had put weight recently, and looked chubby with a round face, but her knotted brow and angry staring eyes looked the same as always, and her face that of a double-dyed villain. She came closer and jolted Manda into the water, "So you are denying, huh?! You bitch! I know exactly what you and that whore are doing. How does she taste, huh? You like it, I can see it in your eyes."

Manda didn't respond but tried to settle herself perching again on the side of the stream. She went on with washing.

"You know what I am going to do?! I will tell Master Koorosh about everything, but wait, I have an idea! I'll tell him that you force yourself on Sahra, that you seduce her and give her drugs to engage her in your depraved affair."

Manda didn't reply. She couldn't keep back the drops of tear rolling down her fair soft cheeks. Soraya knew she had succeeded to make an impression. She gave an insidious smile and like a bird of prey was cheered by her imminent triumph, "Listen very carefully Manda. Don't be an arrant fool! You're a stranger here. You have no one to defend you, you have no friends. No one will stand by your side in case of a wanton outrage. Look at you, you even look different from us! Who has here such blue eyes?!"

A silence prevailed for some moments. Drops of tears continued to run down Manda's face. At a moment she brought herself to say something, faltering, "What do you want?"

Soraya's face looked happier than ever. Was she on the verge of what she was longing for? Her breathing got so heavy Manda could hear it clearly, "I want you to do the same that you do for that lascivious boss of yours. I want you to eat my pussy for hours."

Manda broke into sobbing. Maybe her moans would make Soraya's heart soft? Alas, the children of God are anything but content, or merciful.

Soraya knew that her stance was probably not accepted, but she had yet another trick up her sleeve. She resorted to dangling a carrot in front of Manda, "Listen again Manda, I promise that won't be forever. Believe me I understand that it is hard for you. But please understand that I have also my needs. I haven't had sex with no man for ages, since my dog of a father sold me to Koorosh a few years ago. My everyday life has been washing and cleaning others' dirt since then. I also need some recreation."

"Don't I? Why no one cares about me. I am also human!" Manda finally came to words in the midst of whimpering.

"Manda you should be patient. Patience is the key to any success in life. You are young. The most precious things in life are friends in who you can put your trust. You must learn to make some. If you do what I am expecting now from you I will be your friend."

"I don't need any friends."

"Ok, it seems the young lady is up to being stubborn. Anyway in contrast to you I am patient. Just mull it over, and more, I am just thirty. Sahra is how old? Forty four? Five? Think about it, I am much younger, much prettier. I am sure you will enjoy eating me out. You do enjoy eating out women in the crannies of your heart, don't you? Even if you are straight. I am also straight, but I need the warmth. I need to feel wanted. Some woman's lips on my sex is definitely not as satisfying as a large hard throbbing dick, but still it gives me the warmth."

Manda didn't reply and didn't watch how Soraya receded into the mansion again, unknowing if she'd been convincing.

∞ ∞ ∞

Manda had to hurry to hang the washed clothes from the strings to dry up before other servants had gulped down all the food, and she was thirsty too. Of a sudden, as from nowhere, Sahra appeared behind her, "Oh you are still hanging the clothes," Sahra's tone was kind.

"Yes Madam, after that I am going to go eat." Manda implied she wouldn't have time for another job right away. She had learnt to remain hard and not dance to Sahra's every tune to get the due respect from her as a woman.

Sahra in response smiled softly and asked with kindness, "could you please go to the cellar and bring me a box of books I have put beside the large broken silver mirror. Please, I know you are hungry but Madam

56

Lofateau is waiting and I have to go back to her. I want to show her my books of French literature."

Manda didn't know what to say. Sahra's tone was so charming she couldn't bring herself to say no to her. "I see, I will bring it to you right away. You said beside the mirror, you mean that mirror in the last room of the basement?"

"Yes my dear, you're a gem!" she then approached Manda and kissed her cheek, "I would be lost without you, you are my everything!"

Manda drew in her breath and continued with her work. She then went to the basement to retrieve her boss's books. She went down the dark stairs, but then she realized it was too dark to see anything without a lamp, although it was noon. The basement had no windows at all, and was completely under the ground. She had to go to the kitchen to fetch an oil lamp.

The flickering light of the small old oil lamp was barely enough to reveal the outline of the walls. There were many rooms in the basement. Fear slithered down her back. She'd been always afraid of darkness. Aren't all humans so? Man is afraid of unknown and isn't darkness tantamount to unknownness? Manda shivered as she found her way to the last room. Once at the door of it, she stretched her hand holding the lamp to illuminate the inside of the room as far as possible. The oval long mirror stood there under a thick layer of dust. Opposite it there was a large bed with a long cylindrical pillow on it. It was difficult to see the color in that weak light, but it looked dark red or brown. She neared the bed. She could see stripes of cloth fixed to the headboard on both sides, left and right. What were they for? She turned to the mirror to spot the box Sahra had demanded. She could see no box. She waddled toward the mirror. Maybe the box was behind it. The flame of the lamp flickered more and began to fade. It seemed it was running out of oil. She turned round toward the door and left the room in haste. Her knees trembled out of fear. When she reached the entrance door of the basement to climb the stairs, she found it was shut and locked up. She couldn't believe. Why would have someone locked the door?! She tried again, to no avail: the huge steel door was fixed in its place and didn't move. She screamed. But in this depth and so far the mansion's courtyard no one would hear even the loudest of her screams. While she leaned against the door, she sank slowly toward the ground.

∞ ∞ ∞

She had fallen asleep or unconscious. She couldn't say which one. She also couldn't know for how many hours. The rusted steel door was not visible any longer. The old oil lamp was snuffed out. She felt weary, and hunger was gnawing at every bit of her guts. She touched for the door and pulled at it. It was in vain. Someone had locked it. She felt something, like an insect touching her neck. She swept it but at the moment of its touch with her hand she realized it'd been a giant millipede. She screamed and stood to run for the room at the end of the corridor but bumped the wall. She broke into tears and felt her way with her hands. She passed the first door. How many rooms was there between the entrance and that room? Well, it didn't matter, the door to that room would be in cross direction. She stumbled at times, and when she reached that room got on her all fours to feel the way. She hit the walls several times, but finally reached the bed she'd seen opposite the mirror. She climbed the bed to rest a little. She hoped that no millipedes or spiders were around. She hated spiders. They were disgusting, with all those eight long legs. She was often on the verge of crying but didn't have the power to shed tears. She fell unconscious again.

∞ ∞ ∞

When she opened her eyes again, the room was light. She was so weak she could hardly move her head around, so tried to spot the source of light by only moving her eyes. The source was a tiny window on the top edge of the wall where the headboard abutted. Someone had pulled its cover to a side. She realized her wrists were fixed to the bars of the headboard. A sound of feet thudding the floor alerted her. Someone was coming. She feared for her life, and then Sahra, erect and looking proud as always, appeared at the door threshold. She wore her long ebony frock and had made her hair into a ponytail.

"Sahra!"

Sahra gave a kind smile, "My baby is awake," and then she shambled to the tripod stool she'd placed beside the bed and sat herself on it. "At last you are awake," she sent Manda a kiss through the air.

Manda couldn't realize what had happened. She thought of that box which was supposed to be beside the mirror. "I am happy you're awake. I missed you!"

"I am so thirsty."

"Now you start being selfish again, Manda! We haven't begun talking for one single minute, and instead of asking me how I am you think of your own desires."

To someone with common sense Sahra would sound having gone nuts. Manda however didn't understand what she meant by all this. Why were her hands tied to the bed?

"Manda, I was worrying about you. I told you how much I love you. Be sure I need you as much as you need water."

Manda wanted to beg for water but she was drained. She was almost a corpse. Waves of fear traversed her being. Fear of inability, fear of an imminent darkness.

Sahra produced a book she had hidden under the lap of her dress and flipped through its pages. She read something. She then put the book to a side and altered the way she spoke, without emotions now, "Manda I know you are thirsty. Believe me I really want to bring you some fresh water from that stream you love, but from now on nothing will be free Manda. You should have to deserve it. You should give me something." She then stood up and as she watched Manda's listless eyes undressed slowly. She'd been completely nude under that dress, not even panties. She looked at Manda and moved closer, climbed up the bed and stood above Manda's head looking down on her. Manda already knew what Sahra wanted and watched how Sahra's hips moved down toward her face. Sahra squatted over Manda's face and then with her hand, grabbed her head and fixed her face under her own muff. "Lick! If you want water you need to give me an orgasm!"

Manda was terrified. An orgasm! She knew how long it would take her to make Sahra cum. She didn't have the vigor for that. "Sahra I can't! Please bring me water, then I will try."

"Oh, you're so selfish Manda! Just try."

Manda flicked Sahra's pussy with her tongue, but soon slumped back into the pillow as weakness pulled her down. "Oh you are such a disappointment, Manda!" Sahra sounded really angry. "I will go."

She stood up with a jolt and got down the bed, "You are rubbish Manda! You have only a pretty face and blue eyes, nothing more."

Manda heard how Sahra's footsteps were receding. She went uneasy. She realized she had to fight for a gulp of water. There was no mercy. It was not the time to be stubborn. "Sahra! Sahra! Please come back." Sahra continued walking away, impassive to Manda's imploring. "Sahra, I will make you cum!!!"

The footfalls suddenly stopped, and then Manda took a sigh of relief because of an approaching Sahra. Sahra's face was stoic, "So you changed your opinion?! But I am serious, no orgasm, no water!"

She straddled the Persian girl's face again. Manda began eating her boss's pussy agitatedly. Soon Sahra was moaning. She got wet. Manda was so desperate for water she savored the dampness in her mouth. Sahra set about rubbing her snatch onto Manda's mouth and nose violently. Her nipples got hard and her womanly juice began to trickle down her thighs and on Manda's cheeks. She rubbed her gooch harder onto Manda's beautiful but pounded face, but it was useless. She couldn't cum. It was all too much repeated what they did, the act, the atmosphere, and there had been no foreplay.

Manda was aware Sahra wouldn't cum only by eating her crotch. She knew her boss's temper thoroughly, and what if she couldn't give her what she needed? Fear filled her chest. Time was running out fast. She had to fight in two fronts: remain physically agile and don't let Sahra simmer down again, and come up with an idea to stimulate her more. This made up her mind for her, and parted her mouth from Sahra's privates. Sahra looked down at her. The view of her ruined face and beaten eyes made her heart race. "Ssaaahra," Manda stuttered begging, "I I neeeeed your help."

"What?"

"You rub your clit with your hand, I will lick the rest for you, ok?!"

Sahra was shaking hard and was so excited that she felt chill all over her shaved white body. She nodded and shifted her buttocks a bit forward, and began kneading her own clit forcefully. She felt Manda's tongue tip stroke her labia and perineum. She had goose bumps all over. Her nipples jutted out like two large rose thorns. She shuddered and moaned. Yet she didn't feel that tongue intensively enough. She shouted with a rough voice, "Manda! Harder! I won't repeat!"

Manda did as her mistress had asked of. Sahra unclenched her cheeks for Manda not to lose anything. "All over!"

She kneaded her own clit hard again. She shuddered violently, and hers was long and hard. Sweet ran down her breasts and thighs and into Manda's mouth. She panted, "Thank you Manda, I will bring you fresh water in a while. Just give me some time."

Manda exhaled with relief. She was so glad at the prospect of drinking water. She had deserved it.

∞ ∞ ∞

Having drunk water, Manda had to bear the strikes of a rod Sahra had brought along. She had to grow more obedient and stop arguing with her. Sahra, with a heavy heart and disliking it so much as she'd put it, had to punish Manda for being balky.

"Twenty, twenty one,.." With every stroke, a feeble scream made Sahra yet a bit damper between the legs. Could life become still more beautiful? She doubted. She whispered quietly in Manda's ear, "After 100 I will fetch you a hearty meal my dear. Just hang on." And then, "Twenty two, twenty three,.." and yet, another swift stroke of rod.

CHAPTER NINE: THE TRAPPED INNOCENT

How beautiful the sunrise was! Sigolene loved the reds sun rays painted on the morning sky. She was fascinated when those reds grew brighter, so strong was her love for nature's motifs to color the world. There was but more to that: As an inveterate traveler, she was starkly in need of an anchor at which to find peace in her constantly changing environment. Now in Persia the only scenes familiar to her were at day, the sun and at night, the moon and stars.

She let out a sigh. Life was often trying. Yesterday she had been at Jome Mosque to photograph that adorable structure which was exquisitely decorated with emerald mosaic tiles. Its pair of fifty-seven yards tall minarets were the highest in Persia. They had crowned the mosque's entrance. She was amazed by the glory of that structure when a woman in long chador had arrived out of the blue and talked with a reprimanding tone, "What are you doing here, European woman?"

"I'm just photographing this amazing edifice."

"Are you Muslim?"

"No I'm not, I am Christian. Anyway why are you asking?"

The woman, looking in her mid-fifties, didn't reply, instead she moved her sight toward the strange device on the tripod Sigolene had erected.

"What's this?" It seemed the nosy woman's questions was not going to be put paid to. "This is a camera. We make photos with it."

"Photos?! What are photos?"

Sigolene debated as to how to answer this question. In France most people already knew what photos were, so she didn't have to explain such rudimentary questions to adults. But it dawned on her that about a month ago she had to explain that to a child, "Quickly made painting! Yes, quickly made painting! This device, I mean this thing makes fast paintings of objects, people, animals, things. Instead of posing for a long while, you just ignite the flash powder and then you have the painting sketched quick."

"Can you paint me with it?"

"It is not that simple. The painting doesn't come out right off. I should produce it later in a laboratory, in a dark room."

"Are you a witch?"

Sigolene was both annoyed and afraid, "Lady I am very hungry. I think I leave now." She set about folding the tripod and dismounting the camera to put them in her carryall which she had brought along. As soon as she walked toward the carriage with which she had come here from Sahra's mansion, the woman called out to her, "Don't go that way. Urchins would hurl stones at you there."

"Thank you but the carriage waiting for me is over there."

She lugged the heavy carryall along. Mehran, a young Persian man waited there for her. He was tall, broad-shouldered and had a short beard and a tall forehead. His dark penetrating eyes looked straight under his raven eyebrows. He was so good-looking but taciturn. Sigolene didn't know the reason was he had never talked to a woman except for her own relatives, let alone a European woman who looked conspicuously different from everyone here. As soon as he saw her, Mehran got off the cart attached to two Arabic horses to help Sigolene. They heaved the carryall together onto the cart's freight bed. "It is heavy!" Sigolene laughed and tried to open a conversation, but Mehran's answer was brief, "Yes"

This saddened her. It had been a long time since she'd had a conversation with someone. At least in Tehran there were lots of foreigners and also open-minded Persians who could keep one company, but here in this small town she sometimes felt she was on another planet. The only one with whom she could manage to talk on some subject was that haughty woman Sahra. However, Sigolene couldn't believe how that woman tried to present a westernized image of herself and at the same time treat her servants how people did in Stone Age.

As Mehran prodded the two horses by his goad Sigolene sidled a glance at him. His expression seemed hard. Sorrow seized her wits as she felt lonely after her long working hours. As the cart moved farther along the rutted road in direction of Sahra's mansion, the minarets receded into the dazing shine of the scorching afternoon sun.

∞ ∞ ∞

Sahra enjoyed it so much when Manda sucked her nipples. Was it because she'd never had a child and the arousing feeling was immensely pleasant to her? It had been a week since she had tricked Manda into this basement and had imprisoned her. Manda was at her mercy. Sahra gave her food or water only when she felt like, and Manda had to deserve it, Sahra kept saying. However awful that circumstance for Manda was, it was the best thing that had happened to Sahra.

Only that morning had her husband Koorosh who'd arrived from a long trip to Tehran waken up in an as-usual-sulky mood and with words that rent Sahra's heart. After Sahra had brought him breakfast to bed and had asked him kindly if he had time for her wife to chat a little, and that she had missed him so much, his gruff response had been, "Oh God, it's again morning. It's again morning! And you come the first thing with your nonsense along."

Sahra sucked in her breath, trying hard not to cry. Her self-esteem, or what had remained of it didn't let her cry. She arrived only moments later in the basement where she had chained the hapless Manda to a large old hickory bed, forgetful of the inquisitive Soraya's prying eyes. Was she doing Manda down to make up for her own shattered self-esteem? Manda had waken up only minutes ago to a reality that she still couldn't believe, even after one whole week, confined in a dungeon and in chains.

"Have you brought water? I am thirsty."

"Later, I need your mouth."

Manda didn't argue. She knew it was useless. Sahra undressed herself in such a hurry as if her life was meant to terminate in a few moments and she was there to enjoy every single remaining moment.

"Do you want to sit on my face?"

"No sit up!" Manda was still lying, her head on the long cylindrical dark crimson pillow, "I want you to suck my nipples."

Manda sat up and a naked Sahra cast herself into her embrace, her breasts level with Manda's mouth. "Suck them," her voice was still rough.

Manda took a nipple into her mouth. Soon Sahra was panting and venting her emotions. She grabbed Manda's hand and slipped it to her own privates. "Rub it my love."

Manda stopped sucking Sahra's nipple, "I don't love you Sahra."

Sahra's face looked sad shortly, but she pulled herself together faster than Manda had imagined, "I don't care. Just make me cum. I need it, or there won't be water until tomorrow."

That impassive gesture wracked Manda's face. She obeyed and fingered Sahra's private parts. Soon Sahra was shaking. She embraced Manda tightly and pressed her bosom onto her face for a whole minute. After her body parted from Manda, the latter gasped for air as if been on the verge of suffocation. Sahra needed time to come down, but when she did, her words were devastating, "Manda I don't care any longer if you love me or not. I am a miserable woman. Only half an hour ago my husband cast me out of his bed like rubbish. I need you to make my life worth living. You must accept it. The rest of your life you will be bound to this bed and serve me. This room and I will be the last things you will ever see. So try to accept it. You know what? I have also thought of amusements for you. You can paint pictures of me. I will bring you pencils and colors and I will lie here naked and you make pictures of me."

"That's insane."

"No it's not," Sahra moved closer to Manda and tapped her forehead with her own finger while speaking, "I want to be inside your head, Manda. There shouldn't be anything else. Only me and my body. I want you to know the tiniest furrows of my skin by heart. Believe me in thirty years from now you will know every crease on my body, and will know exactly how every spot tastes. I will be your whole world. I wish this room were smaller, so you would focus still more on me."

Tears shone around Manda's dark lashes in the dim light of the room. "This is inhumane Sahra," her voice wobbled, "I am not your property. Please don't be so cruel to me. I am human like you. Put yourself in my shoes. How can be so rough to someone else?"

"The same reason the whole world is rough on me."

Manda kept her temper in check and held back her tears. Sahra couldn't see that her condition was the same as her own feelings less than only an hour ago, or she saw and didn't care. When Sahra was back in her room, Koorosh had left again.

CHAPTER TEN: THE AMERICAN BUSINESS

Koorosh had been in a hurry. He had an appointment with the head of the chamber of the American business relations in Tehran. He climbed the wide marble stairs to the entrance of the building quick to stay on time. The secretary ushered him into the room where Mr. McKenzie and his wife Linda waited for her. They were there to pull off a huge deal. The company McKenzie Business was going to become the exclusive supplier of Persian pistachio to the United States and Europe.

"Come take a seat," Mr. McKenzie received Koorosh at the door of a large office. Mrs. McKenzie was sitting on an armchair with blue silk cushions across the rather small round hickory table in the middle of the room. She could hold her own with her quite attractive curves visible under her tight dark blue blouse and a skirt which revealed her legs up to her thighs. Koorosh sat himself opposite her. Past her shoulder he could see an expensive ornate mantle clock placed on a shelf. Mr. McKenzie sat beside Koorosh and offered him some red wine.

"Yes please," greedy and ambitious as he was, Koorosh was there to gallop through the negotiations and to cinch the deal. However, as a matter of habit he got engaged in small talk.

"What wine actually is this, Mr. McKenzie?"

"Bordeaux, imported from the land of culture and civilization, France." Mr. McKenzie's intonation was as rhythmic as poetry, "So have you thought about our agreement proposal?"

"Actually I didn't have enough time to think everything over thoroughly. But one thing I can say, most of your requests I can meet."

"Most?!" Mr. McKenzie laughed while pouring wine in the glass in front of Koorosh, "I thought we agreed you will get our so to say, full financial support if you could guarantee the Ministry's agreement on all stipulations."

"But I beg you, I am not in a position to provide you with exclusive rights to buy pistachio in Persia. Russians and British, lately also Germans have also got a lot of influence in this country. My friends in senate won't agree on giving such prerogative to an American company."

Mr. McKenzie's lips twitched and he leaned back to the armchair. As his slim body didn't possess that much volume he almost sank into the seat cushion. He cleared his throat and gave a crooked smile, "Well actually we even didn't ask for exclusive rights for purchase in all of the country. We just pointed to certain provinces, to Yazd and to Isfahan, and also to the capital Tehran."

Koorosh scoffed, "but that's all the area where you could buy high quality pistachios. That is virtually equivalent to exclusive purchase rights in all of country."

Mr. McKenzie clapped his hands once, "I give up. I will go and smoke a cigar. Linda, would you join me?"

Mrs. McKenzie, slouching so far over her glass on the table straightened her torso and put one leg on another. She grinned, "I would not leave Mr. Malard alone. It would not be polite."

Koorosh didn't notice the meaningful expression on Mr. McKenzie's face as he left the room onto the terrace to smoke his cigar. He went down the terrace to sit on a rickety chair with an enough distance from Koorosh that he could barely see his outline past the chair's edges.

"It's a good wine isn't it?"

"Oh yes, Mrs. McKenzie, really good."

"Yes, French wines are always good, especially I love the Bordeaux."

"Do you also have wine made in your country?"

"Well sure. In the United States we also produce wine, but not where I come from, in Nebraska."

"I thought you lived in New York."

"Yes we do. I moved to New York after I got to know Dick, my husband. He runs his business there."

"New York should be an amazing city. I've been to Paris. It was marvelous! Can New York keep up with it?"

"Well they are actually very different cities. Comparing them would be comparing apples and oranges. European cities have an originality and identity American cities lack, such as those magnificent historical buildings which dot Paris, around the Champs-Élysées particularly. But New York's bustling night life beats that of Paris. That myriads of bars and pubs. I really miss it when I travel around. That's such a pity. I don't remember the last time I got dressed to the nines and went to a swanky restaurant, you know, showing some skin, some cleavage, expensive high heels, the works. I miss men's leering eyes."

Koorosh chuckled, "You don't need to mention that when your husband is around," he poured some wine for both of them. He took his in haste.

"No it's ok with Dick. We are quite open minded on subjects related to our personal life."

Koorosh coughed as if the wine had flown the wrong way down his throat, "That's impossible in Persia. If I knew my wife would talk about showing skin to a stranger man, I can't imagine the anger that would overwhelm me."

Mrs. McKenzie smiled, "That's very seldom in the U.S. as well. But sometimes when people get older, they are not as possessive as they used to be before, and I assure you it's just about the conversation to close friends."

A moment went by in silence as they both took a swig of the dainty wine. "My husband told me you are seldom home, in Yazd."

"Really?! He did? I thought I had told you that myself."

71

"Oh I remember. We were at Hilton, right? I think you told me you had often as not arguments with your wife."

Koorosh laughed, "Not only arguments. More like quarrels."

"Well maybe it's because Persian men are overbearing." Mrs. McKenzie took side with the fellow woman she didn't know.

"Oh you are wrong. Persian men are not overbearing, and even if they are what's it to me? I always try to be tender to my wife, but it doesn't work. She doesn't want peace, that's as truthful as the reality."

"You are tender. A tender Persian man is something very especial. I like especial men."

Koorosh was confused why Mrs. McKenzie made advances today. They actually didn't know one another that well, nor were they close friends as she had just put it. They had met on parties four or five times with always her husband being present.

Next moment she reached her hand to softly touch Koorosh's which was holding the glass. "You can talk to me anytime you need to. I am always there for you."

"What do you mean by this? You have a husband to look after," his words were defiant but his fast pace of breathing betrayed his mood at that moment. Linda smelled a whiff of lust.

"The very first time I saw you I said to myself oh, what a dashing handsome man. I had a mild crush on you. Please don't laugh because of my age. Romance doesn't know age. Every time I talked to you my passion for you grew stronger. I want to feel your lips on mine." She briefly pulled at the rim of her skirt to reveal more of her smooth flesh. Koorosh had now a view of her luscious thighs.

"That's enough," Koorosh slammed his fist on the table, "I am sorry. I have to leave."

"You're welcome." Mrs. McKenzie looked a bit afraid. Koorosh stood up, "I do apologize. I'm just afraid of your husband, that's all." He sounded nervous.

"My dear you don't have to be afraid of him. We are now in our villa on Pahlavi Avenue. Dick leaves tomorrow morning for New York, via London. If you like you can come to me and spill the beans, say anything that presses your heart."

"Thank you, I appreciate your attention."

"And Mr. Malard, can we be a little indiscreet?"

"Yes, probably, why?!"

"Women want to be adored. That's why in places where there is freedom they love to show skin as much as etiquette allows them to. Pay attention to your wife. I mean also physically. How you ever tasted her lovely parts?"

Koorosh twisted his face in disgust as he'd caught her drift, "Oh no, you mean that? Never! For her? Yikes!"

"You don't like to do that for her because she is she, or because she is a woman?"

"I don't know. This is a very embarrassing question. I really have to leave now!"

"We will find out!"

At this moment, Mr. McKenzie opened the terrace door to enter the room. Koorosh twirled in surprise. "Mr. McKenzie?! You're back!"

"Yes, are you surprised Mr. Malard? My cigar wasn't that long," McKenzie was witty. They all laughed. Koorosh but collected himself and decided to leave. "Already going Mr. Malard?"

"Oh yes, Mr. McKenzie. I have to run, I have another appointment. Thank you so much for the wine."

"Good bye Mr. Malard, have a wonderful afternoon," Mr. McKenzie didn't bother to escort a scuttling Koorosh to the door.

CHAPTER ELEVEN: THE CRUEL CLOCK

They raised the carryall to the freight bed and climbed up the cart. Sigolene was happy at her accomplishments today: She had photographed the ancient Zoroastrian fire temple and the Zoroastrian priest had agreed that she would take his photo and that of the worshipping congregation. The burning fire had been there for two thousand years he'd said, and was kept alive through centuries by servants of the temple.

She was so cheerful she needed to celebrate her work with someone. She knew that Sahra could provide her with several bottles of Shiraz Wine, it should be delicious. She had tried it several times on occasions in Paris. But she disliked celebrating anything with her.

She broke the silence and asked Mehran where she could find alcohol of any kind in Yazd.

"My lady wine or liquor is difficult to find here. Here the majority are Muslims. If there should be wine you shall find it at the Jew's or the Zoroastrian's."

"Yes but these people certainly have their own shops where they trade alcohol too?!"

"No my lady, it is prohibited."

"Oh" Sigolene sighed. Moments later, Mehran looked at her with a smile she hadn't seen of him thus far, "I will bring you a bottle. I know someone."

"How much does it cost?"

"I think around two rials."

Sigolene wanted so much to share her feelings with someone, "You know today I am so happy."

"You look happy! That's why you need the drink, right? To celebrate."

"Oh, you read my mind. I like you being talkative. Why aren't you usually?"

"My lady I don't know if I am allowed to talk to you. I am a vassal and you are a woman of noble lineage."

"Who's said that I am from a noble lineage? Did Sahra say? I'm not."

"You look like one."

"So you decide it by the looks of someone?"

Mehran kept his look on the stony road.

"I allow you to talk Mehran."

"How can you allow?! You are a woman. Your husband is supposed to allow."

"Huh?!" Sigolene shouted in disbelief, "only a few seconds ago I was an aristocrat, and now I'm just a woman, you're nuts. You know what, you don't have to speak. Just keep your mouth shut!"

Mehran looked at her with sorry eyes, "My lady I didn't mean to insult you. This is how I learnt it. I thought also in your culture, and where you come from, a husband must allow a woman to talk to another man."

"No in France, where I come from, no woman is obliged to ask her husband for permission for such trivial matters. Thanks God. And just for you to know I am not married."

Now Mehran's look was that of a wondering man, "How is that possible at your age and with your beauty?"

Sigolene laughed, "Yes, my age. Now are you married? How old are you?"

"I am twenty two. I am unfortunately still unmarried because I own nothing, no cows, no camels, no land. My mother has asked many fathers for their daughters' hand for marriage with me. All rejected. They said they didn't want to ruin their daughter's life."

"Do you even know those women?"

Mehran cleared his throat and squared his shoulders while goading the right horse with his stick once again, "No, but I don't have to. My mother knew them. I trust her more than I trust myself."

"I imagined so. Do you know what love is? You never thought of loving a woman first, and then marrying her, did you?"

"I know what love is. I know it from poetry and tales. Farhad loved Shirin, and Majnoon loved Leili. I believe in love, and I know I will fall in love after I marry."

Sigolene gave him a tight-lipped smile, "Yes that's a good strategy. It relieves you from the investment of finding love yourself, what I failed to achieve so far. However, did you know those lovers were not married to their beloved ones in those stories?"

No answer came. Hadn't he heard what she just spoke? She tugged on her jacket lapel nervously. Her eyes took a slow slide down his body. He wore an old suit which lay tight on his body, and could barely conceal his powerful build. He exuded masculinity. She so much craved for such a muscular arm to grab her body and hold her tight, like an anchor in her stormy sea of life. But the owner must be someone who loved her. Alas, that man couldn't even grasp what the real meaning of love was. "So you didn't know that those lovers were not married, did you? I've been studying Persian Literature for a long time. I bet you can't even read." She insisted.

"I do. I read literature, and I know stories who you certainly have never heard of, and they are much more erotic than Shirin and Farhad or Leili and Majnoon."

"Erotic, you even know the word! So tell me one of those erotic stories, I am burning to hear it from a Persian."

77

"I prefer not to relate it in front of a lady."

"No you do! Well, if you need again permission, yes I allow you to relate, and I trust you. You don't look like someone who goes naughty in the middle of an erotic story and rapes a lonely woman in the middle of a desert and at that, on a shabby dray."

"Have you ever heard of the story of Princess Irandokht?"

"Princess who? Oh that name is really Persian? Not so straightforward like Shirin or Majnoon, but no! Complicated! Irandokht!" Sigolene stressed the last word in a mocking way.

"You Europeans are arrogant. You look beautiful, but your heart is that of an overbearing person. If you don't know Princess Irandokht, you don't have to scoff and ridicule our language and culture. Instead, you could remain silent and try to learn something that you probably don't yet know."

"Ok, educate me. Tell me the story of Princess Irandokht."

"There was a time when Persia was an Empire reaching the Shores of the Mediterranean Sea in the west and the splendid peaks of Himalayas to the east, were glaciers dotted the mountainous landscape. In that era the Empire was ruled by a vigilant wise Emperor, whose might and splendor was the talk of every highbrow session. His name was King of Kings, Khosrow Parviz. Khosrow Parviz was not only a valiant warrior and a shrewd politician, but also a fertile father. He had many daughters and sons, and that only of two wives: Shirin and Mary."

Hearing this Sigolene exploded in laughter. Color flooded Mehran's face.

"I am sorry! I didn't mean to laugh. Please go on."

"One of those daughters was Irandokht, the daughter of Mary, a princess who had married the Emperor of Persia from the Byzantine Roman Empire. Irandokht was as beautiful as Mary, that's to say, her grace was utterly breathtaking. Her sea-blue eyes would overwhelm every beholder, her scent would inebriate the most impassive of hearts.

Her legs were so shapely as if God Almighty had spent half of his time to mold those magnificent forms, and the other half the rest of the world.

"But often it's the same story with man, if they have something in excess, no matter riches or beauty, they lack others such as modesty and humanity. Irandokht was not only arrogant and opinionated, but she was the most jealous of all her dynasty. Soon she undertook secret ventures to subvert the rule of her father and marginalize her siblings. She was up to claiming the throne. Her father but was on to her soon. He loved her daughter, and instead of punishing her he sent her to a peculiar exile: He gave her the Yazd Governorate as a gift. She wasn't but happy with that. As soon as she set foot on the parched ground of Yazd she vowed to rule the town and its surroundings with an iron feast. She was to wreak her vengeance on innocent subjects. On the very first day, the tax collectors were informed if their contribution was not going to sum up to the level required by the court, their head would be added to the tribute to make good. She held her word. Only six months later the majority of the darughachis, the officials in charge of taxes, were decapitated. The Empress commanded to put the heads on spikes and put them on display, so they would be a lesson for the other disobedient. The Princess was but not only a woman of indignance, on occasions she also showed mercy, but one of a very particular nature. I don't know if you want to hear that? It would be indiscreet the words I am going to say."

"Sure, it's just words. I'm interested."

"Irandokht loved an especial type of satisfaction. Man would worship her private parts, and that was the basis on which she made up her mind. She had built a device by an engineer from Kerman. The name of the engineer was Harmoozd. It was a type of double-barreled clock. A very strange type of one, armed with a large steel blade. The convicted was placed on a stool, a wooden plane with a hole in it was floating above his head. There sat the princess. He had to please her with his mouth until she was satisfied. If she was he would come out in one piece. However, there was a catch: It shouldn't have lasted more than half an hour. That was when the clock triggered the blade to chop off the hapless guy's head."

79

"That's disgusting. Where have you read this? I don't believe someone would put this down in history. Especially in a place like here. You've concocted that all by yourself, haven't you?"

"Read the book Hazaliyat of Sa'adi, it's all there."

"I can't believe Sa'adi has written such nonsense."

Sigolene averted her look from Mehran and viewed the desert sunset. She wanted to find peace in the scenery and forget the cruel story she'd just heard. However, what she'd never expected, her nipples had pebbled to hard buds and her privates had gone wet. Was it because she was so fond of stories of strong women? She remembered how much she had enjoyed reading about the life of Russian Empress, Catherine the Great, and the way she was surrounded by numerous lovers, many of whom had lost their lives because of Empress's political decisions on keeping up appearances and avoiding the throne from being stained by unpleasant news. She looked at Mehran again. She wanted him to devour her. What a beautiful mouth he had. What a thrilling story she'd just heard. Disgusting and thrilling at the very same time.

CHAPTER TWELVE: THE OASIS

Today they were riding to a nearby fortress. The Abrandabad Fortress was built by Irandokht. Sigolene had a strange feeling upon riding to that castle. The story of the bladed clock had left its trace on her. At first she had thought it loathsome, but wasn't that woman the epitome of female strength?

If they'd known, it would be devastating for her friends back in France to know that her mind entertained such thoughts, but she just imagined the power that cruel Persian woman had felt in that moment, and how desperate that man should have been, and her hair rose on the back of her neck. A man who in those last moments of life had one mere destination, a pure unadulterated one, to hear the sound of orgasm of a despotic woman who was in power, for her to disable that murderer gadget.

∞ ∞ ∞

The hilly sandy landscape looked a reddish orange that made one feel hot. Under her long dress and straw hat Sigolene was sweating. If she had been alone she would have taken off that dress, but on the other hand the sun would singe her skin for sure. Mehran was also breathing fast out of the heat. He sidled at the French woman.

"It is too hot for you, isn't it?"

"Yes it is."

"Where you come from it must be much colder I assume."

"Oh yes, but where I come from, France, is even warmer than many parts of Europe, such as Germany or Sweden. But here is still not comparable."

"Yes, this scorching sun always hovers over us in the sky. You won't believe how hot it could get here. I once cooked eggs on a flat black stone. The heat was enough."

81

"Yes, and that's why you got that beautiful deep tan."

"Deep tan, what do you mean with that?"

"Your skin is so dark, look at mine. It is white usually, now it is ruby red for the heat."

"But I think your skin is much prettier. Your hands have the color of snow. It's so scarce here."

"I don't believe, you know what snow is? Do you have snow here?"

Mehran threw his shoulders momentarily back and adopted a proud tone, "Yes, in Persia we have snow. Especially in the northern parts. But here in Yazd it may snow in deep winter every couple of years once. So white is really scarce here to come by."

"Did I tell you that you are everything my former boyfriend wasn't? Dark, tall, broad across the shoulders. Your comparison just reminded me of him. He also liked fair women."

Mehran chuckled, "Having a large frame is normal here. Life is so hard we don't afford not to have broad shoulders and brawny arms. Those who don't have, would not survive their childhood."

"I won't believe that. I haven't seen anyone in Yazd having impressive a frame as you have yet."

A grin appeared across Mehran's face. Sigolene couldn't believe, "You were kidding me?! Oh you're unbelievable! How could you do that to me?!" Mehran laughed out loud. The invisible barrier between them was melting away.

"You know Sigolene, you are such a modest person. I had thought Europeans must be haughty, but it is heart-warming to talk to you. I really enjoy your companionship. You don't look down on people around you."

"Although I am rich," she gave a crooked smile, "It's so hot here, oh thank you."

The vehicle was approaching a fork. An idea dawned on Mehran. "Look there. The left way runs to the Abrandabad Fortress, the right to an oasis with trees and a small pond. If you like we can rest there a bit and then ride to the fortress."

"How far is that?"

"Only one mile. You will see the trees if we get past that hill," Mehran held out his hand to point at a hill close to the fork.

"And how far is it to the fortress?"

At least eight more miles.

Although it was getting late in the afternoon, Sigolene couldn't contain herself, "So let's get to that stand."

At the fork, Mehran pulled the bridle and prodded the horses in that direction. Sigolene couldn't take her eyes off this rube. No matter how primitive his appearance was, and how far he'd lapse into that awkward slouching pose went, he looked attractive to her. Maybe the reason was that she liked original things, and this unsophisticated, simple man was as pristine as the old Yazd which she'd been craving much to photograph for so long.

No sooner did she snap out of her reverie than her brute friend shouted loud to stop the horses. They had reached the stand. A small pond with clear blue water shimmered behind the row of cedar trees. "Here we don't have palms do we?"

"No not in Yazd," Mehran jumped down and held Sigolene's hand as she dismounted the cart, "although in summer here it's really hot, in winter the weather may reach freezing temperatures which palms don't hold out."

"You know you have a kind of plummy way of talking. Are you sure you're illiterate?" Sigolene landed on both her feet and let a cloud of dust rise.

"My lady when did I say that I was illiterate?! Have you already forgotten our small debate as to Persian literature? Does an illiterate know how to read Sa'adi's poetry?"

"Stop calling me 'my lady.' Call me by my first name."

"Which is?"

"Oh I don't believe. You don't know it yet?! That's when you always treat people so obsequiously. A man like you who also reads literature as you claim must also keep a minimum level of self-esteem."

"Why?"

"What do you mean why? Like when someone is educated, he will not fawn all over everyone else. That's just normal."

"And if he's hungry?"

"Well that will never happen. Because if someone is learned and knowledgeable, they will never starve."

"Well I went to the American school in Isfahan, and I got my highschool degree there, and after that I was still hungry. When I was graduated I learned that that degree by itself won't bring anything, and that I had to go to university in Tehran to get a higher degree so as to be able to get a job. I didn't have money to go to Tehran, so I returned to Yazd. I am lucky I can work for Mr. and Mrs. Malard as a chauffeur. Otherwise I were probably dead now!"

"You went to the American school in Isfahan?! What did they teach you there? Can you speak English? French?"

"English yes, French no."

Sigolene drawled, "Oh that's funny. Because I am European but I know no English. But you are here in the middle of an unforgiving desert and you know it. Amazing!"

They went through the thicket that had popped up in the middle of that dry desert and reached the pond. Sigolene went blissfully, "Oh my goodness, how clear this water is! Are there any fish inside?"

"No, but baby frogs, and frogs."

They both squatted down and scooped up water with their cupped hands to drink and wash their faces and arms. The cool water originated from an underwater spring. "I would like to swim inside another time."

"You can swim now if you want. I will go over to the cart and take rest in the shadow of the horses. You can undress and swim as long as you'd like."

Before Sigolene could appreciate the Persian man's propriety he had walked away to the horses. Sigolene looked around carefully to make sure there were no prying eyes among surrounding bushes and trees. She took off her shoes, blouse and trousers, even her panties. She hadn't been wearing a bra. She entered the chilly water which was soon going to restore her drained sap. She swam along the pond to the corner where the vast desert was still visible through a hole into the high growth of weeds. She felt somehow safe here. She looked in the direction of the horses and could make out the lying silhouette of Mehran. The next moment, she was diving underwater. She loved the feeling of moving suddenly from air to water, from one medium to another. She turned over and looked at the sky from inside the water. She could see the warped forms of the trees encircling the pond.

Mehran thought shortly of prying on the beautiful French woman but he averted his eyes away from the pond and fought down his desire. He hated if people thought he wasn't reliable. He lay in the shadow of those horses and looked at the blue sky.

"I wish it would rain soon. The ground is all too thirsty." He was out cold as soon as his head hit the palms of his closed hands.

∞ ∞ ∞

He was started when he heard a loud shrill cry. "Help! Help!" It took him a moment until he remembered where he was. He stood up to see

85

Sigolene from afar, who was completely naked, crying in fear. He forgot his shame and ran to see what had happened. He saw Sigolene, all wound up, was encircled by a bunch of desert tarantulas. "Don't move! They will jump at you if you move!"

"Please help me Mehran!" Sigolene tried to hide her crotch with her hands as she shook out of fear.

"Easy! Just come down!"

He took a thick branch lying nearby and moved it near the first tarantula. As soon as it jumped at the thick branch, he squashed it by a firm blow on a nearby stone. The trick worked well. He went after every tarantula, one after the other. "They're finished now."

Sigolene had lost control. She jumped, all naked, into Mehran's arms while he still held the branch. "Thank you, I was so afraid!" She sobbed.

Mehran was embarrassed. It was a situation he didn't know. A nude woman shaking in his embrace, but humanity got the better of wonder in his heart and he hugged the woman tightly and gave her the warmth she needed at that moment. Sigolene raised her head to watch Mehran's face and look the Persian man in the eyes. No sooner had their eyes met, than their lips touched. "What are we doing?"

"We are kissing." Sigolene gasped while Mehran did something he didn't even know, yet enjoyed. Soon the hot torrid sun made her anguish evaporate and her lust come about. She parted her body from Mehran's and fixed his eyes with a stern gesture. Mehran tried to hug her again but she held out her arm with an open palm to make distance. Mehran took it as a sign of rejection and made for turning around to go to the cart but Sigolene spoke with an overbearing tone.

"Sahra told me you are a good servant. So tell me, what does a good servant do best?"

"Obey whatever their master says."

"Lie on the grass."

"What?"

"You heard me! I won't repeat!"

Mehran lay on the ground. Sigolene was still somewhat hesitant but she finally mustered her courage. She stood above Mehran's face and kneeled on the ground to sit on the man's face. She was shaking. "Eat me! Please!"

Was it a matter of instinct? Or was it because of the stories he'd read in literature and his own imagination? The rustic vassal sucked her as though he'd had practice for years. He proved to be worthy of it, and patient. It took long. She felt being a queen. She had never had something like this in open air. The touches of Mehran's lips and teeth sent waves of pleasure through her body. How long had she been depraved of such pleasure? She couldn't remember. Eventually, Sigolene noticed that he had got hard. Moments later, upon her signal, Mehran lay her on the ground and pounded her pussy frantically. They moaned while both touching and playing with her breasts, Mehran repeatedly biting at them.

CHAPTER THIRTEEN: THE UNFORGIVING WORLD

Sigolene sat beside the stream. She contemplated how it snaked into the dunes of drifted sand. The past weeks had seen a lot of changes to her life, as well as to the state of affairs of the land she'd come to visit, even the whole world. She traced her own torso all the way up to her neck remembering how last night Mehran had stroked her skin with his warm tongue and had kissed all along the way. He had been so tender to her, and at times, as soon as she had asked of, as rough as a brute, filling her every opening with a hard penis.

When back in Europe, she would miss this man so much! Had it been all along a big mistake? She heaved a deep sigh. How could she take the Persian man with herself back to Europe? There was no legal means. And she could never think of staying in Persia to live with him. She cursed herself for her recklessness.

It had been only a few hours since they had last met, yet she already missed him. She watched the breathtaking but barren scenery stretching up to the distant Zagros Mountains and pondered with a heavy heart. Suddenly a voice brought her out of her daydreaming.

"Mrs. Lofateau?"

She turned around to see a tall man with a long mustache in an attire like a military uniform and a pistol in an old-looking leather holster. The man's dress was a homogeneous khaki color. A metal emblem of a lion, carrying a sun representing the royal government glistered in the light of the sun in front of his cap.

"I am Officer Sasan Morshedi. I am an officer of the royal security forces. Actually I am the sheriff around here."

Sigolene was afraid of the man. "Do you want to check my documents? I have left them inside my room..."

"No that's not why I am here. I wanted to ask you if you know anything about the recently vanished woman servant here, Manda Aghajari."

"Yes, she was a nice girl. Very beautiful. She had those sea-blue eyes you would fall in love with."

"I am not here for her sea-blue eyes. I just want to know what you know about her."

"Well Sahra says she's gone back to her hometown without saying goodbye."

"Yes I have heard that story. However I find it strange that no one knew of that except her. That old woman, Omme Salameh, said they had no good relationship, Sahra and she."

"Yes, but I think Sahra has generally no good relationship to any servant. She's very bossy you know."

"Yes, these aristocrats treat people like rubbish. But the era of their arrogance will end soon. I know that the owner of this mansion has ties to the Qajar dynasty. But now a new dynasty has the reigns. Someday we will come after these folks." The policeman cleared his throat to continue, "Anyway how can you speak Persian so well? How long have you lived here? If you are going to live here forever you must register in the sheriff station near the Jome Mosque. Actually that's why we know of Manda Aghajari, because we wanted to register all the residents and they said one servant had gone missing."

"I have been here for only around a month now. I have learnt Persian at university, in Paris. I am a journalist."

"A journalist?! Have you got permission from the Ministry of Communications?"

"No, I don't. I have been in Persia several times and never needed such a document."

"How you taken photographs?"

"Yes, many."

"Where did you take them?"

"Like several of the Jome Mosque, or of the Abrandabad Fortress. Of an oasis near the Abrandabad Fortress..."

"Have you made photographs of camels?"

"Of course! They are adorable animals in my opinion. They epitomize nature's power to combine seemingly contradictory properties, beauty and self-sufficiency," Sigolene sounded enthusiastic.

"Yes, but photographing camels has been banned by the central government. You were not allowed to do that. We have since one year a new King in Tehran. New king, new rules. He wants to present a new modern image to the world, not an archaic one, and camels are a symbol of a backward nation. Do you have time, the day after tomorrow? You must come over to the police station and declare whatever photos or interviews you've made."

"I can't show you the pictures. I need especial chemicals to make them appear."

"So just make a list. Write them down with a small description for each. See you at the police station the day after tomorrow then, around noon. And Mrs. Lofateau..."

"Miss Lofateau," Sigolene found it important to correct the sheriff.

"Excuse me, Miss Lofateau, if you don't toe the line you will face the music, remember that!"

∞ ∞ ∞

King Reza Shah Pahlavi had recently taken over the reigns in the capital Tehran and had begun altercations with world powers, accusing them of meddling in Persia's affairs. Consulates and politicians from the U.S., Great Britain, France and the U.S.S.R. were no longer welcome in Golestan Castle. Instead he sought proximity to Germany as an

91

alternative to build up the new glorious Persia. Reza Shah had already ordered the closure of the chamber of American business relations in Tehran. When Koorosh arrived in front of Mr. and Mrs. McKenzie's villa on Pahlavi Avenue, he was nervous and excited. Oblivious of the new news and the fact that Americans would not be granted running business in the country any longer. He had thought so much about his call at the attractive American wife's place while her husband would be away for several days. He was thirty and something, but his thoughts were comparable to that of a juvenile who'd going to lose virginity and get it on for the first time in his entire life.

He'd put on his most expensive suit and perfumed himself with costly French eau de cologne to make an impression on the American woman from Nebraska.

Linda McKenzie of course had not forgotten her own invitation of the Persian man, but had lost business interest in him. She as the wife of the chief of the chamber of the American business relations in Tehran had got wind sooner than anyone else of the coming political storm which was meant to uproot the American influence in the country for many years to come, but she had not issued a cancelation yet. Why? Was she curious? Maybe. It was never supposed to go this way. It had been her husband's idea to lure Koorosh into the house. Make him drunk and insist that he would sign an instrument which transfers all his own rights to buy pistachio in Persia to Mr. McKenzie's company. However with the news that the operation of American companies would soon be banned across the country and they will soon be substituted by German operators, what would the use of such an instrument be?

Mrs. McKenzie was drinking tea on the balcony on the second floor overlooking a large apple and pomegranate garden and basking in the scent of the jasmines grown just under the balcony. The chirping of birds and nightingales together with a balmy breeze blowing from the nearby Alborz Mountains elated her soul and filled her with exhilaration. She watched how the vapor left the surface of water in her cup in random patterns. Fatima, the servant, appeared the next moment to announce the arrival of a businessman, "My lady, Mr. Malard has arrived at the entrance. He says he has an appointment with you."

"Yes, usher him to the balcony."

"My lady should I tell him he should wait for you to change?" The servant asked so as Mrs. McKenzie wore a short skirt which barely concealed her panties while seated and a light top with a deep V-neck which was sexy and showed off her breasts and cleavage. Her beauty was accented by a gold necklace with the outline of a heart dangling at its end.

"No, Mr. Malard is like a brother to me. Just usher him in and after that bring him a cup of tea." She ignored the servant's big wondering eyes.

When Koorosh arrived on the balcony, Mrs. McKenzie was clever to attention how he spied her bare flesh while trying to conform to the etiquette, as though he had lost control on his supposedly furtive looks. "Mr. Malard, I have been waiting for you the whole day. Where have you been?"

"Well actually we hadn't set an exact hour for my call, so I just tried to arrive late enough not to disturb you while eating lunch at noon."

"Oh, well, I'd say it's just as well that it's been this way, because my lunch has been quite scant. I think our Persian cook thinks a woman must consume food half as much as a man. Since Dick's been off to New York, the volume of our lunch has fallen by at least two thirds."

"Well maybe you should have a talk to with him."

"I maybe would. But at the same time I'd like so much to keep the volume of this belly in check, so I will debate a little more before I do so," she pointed to her own belly while trying to be all casual.

"May I take a seat?"

"Sure! I'm sorry I didn't offer."

Fatima brought a small glass of tea with a drawing of a Qajar King on it on a tray and put it on the table in front of Koorosh. "Look at this!"

Koorosh looked enthusiastic, "You serve tea with traditional Persian art pieces?!"

Mrs. McKenzie drawled as her tone remained kind, "Oh yes, I love this cute kitchenware I bought several months ago in the bazaar near to the Sadeghieh Square."

"This is a picture of Qajar King. You know that?"

"Yes I do. I had asked the vendor about it."

"I hope King Reza will not ban them. He's an arch enemy of the Qajar Dynasty."

This sentence reminded Mrs. McKenzie again of the fact that Koorosh-himself a relative of Qajars-being there to pay a visit was now useless as to business. "Do you need to drink anything else Mr. Malard? Well as you can see we have already a bottle of gin at hand on the table and a glass for you. Otherwise I will dismiss Fatima."

"No I'm fine. I don't need anything else. Thanks!"

Mrs. McKenzie turned to Fatima who still stood there watching them curiously. She spoke in an arrogant tone while frowning to cow her, "Fatima, now please leave me and Mr. Malard alone and don't come back! Don't let anyone to come to us either."

Fatima obeyed meekly. "Yes my lady."

After she'd left a smile played on Mrs. McKenzie's lips as if to imply how fast the behavior of the servant had turned obsequious, "It's strange. Fatima gets cheeky often as not but I can subdue her quick by simply giving her a stern gesture."

"Well you have got the hang of the Persian culture! In the east we try to remain kind to others and behave gently even if we dislike them. A single wrinkling of the brow here makes the impression of a whole dressing down elsewhere."

"Oh that reminds me of Japanese culture. Have you ever been in Japan so far, Mr. Malard? Or may I call you Koorosh? You can call me Linda if you won't object."

"No not at all. Call me Koorosh. With pleasure! No, sorry. I am certainly not as traveled and knowledgeable of the world as you are."

Mrs. McKenzie gave a smile, "Yes, actually no, you are just being modest. Anyway Japanese behave somehow similar to Persians. They laugh even if treated unfairly. They are used to obey and they are happy with it."

Mrs. McKenzie adjusted herself on the chair and sat so that Koorosh could see most of her skin under her miniskirt. She smiled flirtatiously, "So tell me about yourself Koorosh. How is everything? Last time we spoke you said it was not going well with your wife."

Koorosh twisted his face to a grimace. "I didn't come here to talk about my wife actually!"

"Why are you here then?" Mrs. McKenzie retorted.

Koorosh found he had blurted out the wrong words. He couldn't say anything to make the moment less disconcerting.

"I see! So you are here just to pay a visit. I assume you are here because you want to tell me some secret."

Koorosh couldn't say a word. He was flabbergasted, so Mrs. McKenzie went ahead, "I remember last time you told me you don't like to go down on your woman."

Koorosh's nape hair stood on end. "Yes," he gasped.

Mrs. McKenzie gave a victorious smile, "and now I suppose I can guess why we are sitting here. Last time we met we said we wanted to find out if you don't like giving head to a woman in general, or if you just don't like to do it for your own wife."

Koorosh didn't look vexed this time. No matter how much he was a disdainful macho towards women in general, he would do anything to take those few clothes off the body of the sexy lady who was but a couple of years older, however curvy and well-endowed with shaved white legs that Koorosh wanted to devour. Mrs. McKenzie followed his line of sight which was incident on her panties. "I am very curious to find the answer!" She teased.

"I'd love to give head to you!"

Now they both were breathing fast. Mrs. McKenzie pictured the Persian man lying naked on bed, his penis erect, hard and throbbing, piercing her vagina and filling it to the hilt. The imagination was painful but lusty. She exhaled for a moment and snapped out of her thoughts. Of course she knew it was useless to seduce Koorosh as the new state politics had shattered any hopes of getting trade right privileges as an American. However it was still an opportunity for her to prove to herself that she was still attractive, to a man maybe not that educated and classy but yet hunky. She didn't care if that muscular build with brawny shoulders was mindful of women or respectful to them, she wanted that tongue inside that mouth to land on her crotch, but a price must be paid. She was worth a lot, but what should she ask in return for sex, now that no instrument on vesting exclusive purchase rights had to be signed?

"Go on!" She said while acting on impulse. In her heart she was not willing to deliver her body so easily to the young man.

"Here? You want me to give you head here?"

"Kneel in my front!" Mrs. McKenzie shivered reaching out her hand for Koorosh to kiss. Koorosh sank to the floor in front of her and kissed her hand several times with affection. What was happening? He didn't know such behavior of himself but that woman had so much charm and appeal that it reminded him of the story of Shirin and Farhad, when King Khosrow had asked Farhad to move a mountain to win Shirin. This woman was so beautiful and her skin was so silky smooth and hairless. Of course he didn't know that in contrast to Persian women, European and American women had access to safety razor and could regularly shave their legs. He thought Mrs. McKenzie was completely different.

Mrs. McKenzie stretched her leg and Koorosh grabbed her lower leg and kissed it. He then stroked his fingers up her thigh as she shivered and grunted. He ran his hand up and down her thigh several times and shortly he got bold enough to touch her up her thigh just near her privates. She smiled which urged him on to proceed. Next time he touched her underwear while they both panted. He reached for its waist to pull the panty off but now Mrs. McKenzie batted his hand away. He was but impudent and tried again, but she flicked his hand off her thigh for a second time. "What's the matter?" Koorosh's expression looked puzzled. "No I can't let you do this, I'm sorry. I am married. This is hard for me."

"Why? I thought you like it, and you said your husband wouldn't care. Oh I would do anything for you if you let me take that off."

"Anything?"

"Anything!" Koorosh's response was affirmative.

"Give me a nice present. Something worthy, something that catches my attention and enthralls my heart."

Koorosh looked at her face for a moment. He had thought of something, that much she could say. She had caught a glimpse of decision in his eyes, and now she made up her mind. "Another time! You will go down on me another time!" She adjusted herself on the rickety wooden chair as it creaked.

"Oh no! Please!" Koorosh's insistence was useless. Mrs. McKenzie rolled her eyes as she lighted a cigarette. "My husband will be away for a month. You have one month to give me something convincing of your love to me. In that case I will be all yours, and with all I mean all!"

Koorosh stood up from that awkward position to sit on the chair opposite Mrs. McKenzie. He gave a faint smile and nodded to signal his consent with what she had just requested. Mrs. McKenzie exhaled audibly as she poured some gin for herself.

CHAPTER FOURTEEN: THE PRICE OF CURIOSITY

Sigolene could not sleep that night. The buzzing of mosquitoes had been a constant disruption. The mosquito net Sahra had given her had apparently huge holes, or at least large enough to let those annoying creatures fly inside. She had tried a hundred times to spot the holes to patch them but that had been in vain. In addition, she had the feeling the air was not going to cool off. She stood up from the bed and paced the room up and down a few times. She was uneasy. She stopped by the window and opened its wooden frame to breathe in some fresh air and soothe down. As soon as the window was open, the scenery of the desert night sky revealed itself to her lazy eyes with all its captivating beauty. Hundreds of stars hung from the heaven's ceiling, enough to light up the night in the absence of the moon. Was it a good idea to take a walk? Maybe so she would refresh her mind and come back with a light soul and ready to sleep. She put on her night gown and sandals and shuffled out of the room into the courtyard trying to make no noise. A cool breeze blew. She walked toward the willow tree to better watch the rustling leaves and branches of the solitary tree at the pond. From under the branches and through the vacillating leaves, it looked as if the stars twinkled more often and played a game of hide and seek.

She snapped out of her thoughts when she saw a movement out of the corner of her eye. Someone scuttled down the courtyard toward the backdoor. Her back and the way of swinging her hips was a telltale of who she was: Sahra. "Sahra! Sahra! Where are you going?"

Sahra didn't take notice of the weak voice calling her. The silhouette hurried toward the backdoor opening to the field where you could go to the basement on the left side and could see the silver stream running down the dunes if you looked straight. Sigolene chased Sahra toward out back. She scurried to the stream but she couldn't make out that silhouette in the dark of the night any longer. She turned around and couldn't see anything, but she heard a click. She saw the stairs running down to the basement beside the cistern she so much wanted to photograph but Sahra had prohibited. She walked to the staircase warily. She could see the large metal door was a crack open. "Sahra! Are you there?" No response came. What was Sahra doing in that basement? She was dying to see what was inside, especially after Sahra had been so insistent that she didn't get near there or the adjoining cistern. She went down the stairs just to steal a peep inside. It was such a rare opportunity. She had tried to open that huge iron door several times when no one was around but it was always locked. She pushed the door a little to widen the opening. A candle shimmered on the dirty basement wall, bright enough only to outline the corners and edges. She tiptoed inside. She could hear people murmuring in the room at the end of the corridor. She pricked up her ears. Sahra was not alone. She was talking to someone. A woman. Sigolene was sure. She walked down the corridor very smoothly to make no sound. Close enough, she could now understand Sahra's words.

"Manda I love you so much. You are my everything. I am so sorry that you can't accept that you don't belong to me."

So Manda was being kept captive by Sahra! A shudder of fear ran down Sigolene's spine. Petrified, she listened.

"Sahra why do you insist?! Of course I don't belong to you. You're insane that's why you can't accept that. You cannot hold people in confinement and expect that they will love you someday. I will never love you Sahra!"

"Oh stop!" Sahra gave a vexed yell, "you always force me to punish you. You see it is your own fault. Stand up!"

Moments later the sound of lashes on Manda's body and her screams made Sigolene's hair stand on end. Tears welled up in her eyes but she stifled any sobs. "You are so ungrateful Manda! I love you so much and you keep hurting me."

After a while no squealing could be heard. The basement turned as silent and quiet as a graveyard. Then Sigolene heard Sahra striding toward the door. She swiftly saught cover in the nearest room on the floor. She was lucky; the room didn't have a door, so she could hide fast behind the wall. She heard how Sahra receded and then locked the door.

She remained still for a few moments to be on the safe side. She heard Manda whimper in the other room. She was still hesitant, but ultimately found enough courage to go to her. She opened the door cautiously, as if it was still possible that Sahra would crop up inside. The scene she was confronted with was heart-breaking. Manda lay there, but looked much thinner than a couple of weeks ago Sigolene had last seen her. Manda raised her head to see the woman in the weak flickering light of the candle. "Sahra, are you back again?"

"No, this is Sigolene, Sigolene Lofateau!"

Sigolene barely knew the woman, but a moment later she leaped forward to embrace her in her arms. Manda sobbed, "Thanks God you are here!"

"What's happening here?"

"This crazy woman is gratifying her desires with me. Her husband treats her meanly and she wreaks her fury on me. I felt so alone."

Sigolene hugged her even tighter and stroked her hair. "My dear, I will bring you out!"

Suddenly Manda stopped crying and moved her head from Sigolene's bosom and eyed her with a wondering expression, "How do you want to do that? She has certainly locked the door. You are also trapped, like me."

Sigolene was speechless for a moment. Was Manda right? Should she fight Sahra when she was back again? Sahra was not taller but much stronger than her, and apparently, given how Manda looked like at the moment much more violent and heartless. Was there anything in the cellar which she could use as a weapon to beat her up and get the better of her? She put Manda's head back on her own chest and caressed her. She thought no matter how much sad Manda's face was, her eyes remained incredibly beautiful. She had lusted after this woman a lot, although she'd been only a servant with ragged clothes. It tore her heart to see that adorable girl end up in a dungeon like that. She'd seen a lot of unfairness in her life, but none could come close to this.

She wanted to see that beautiful face again, the face she'd once mentioned looked royal in front of Sahra, and had perceived Sahra's clear resentment of her comment. She gently turned around the head of the Persian woman with her hand to see her face. Their gazes locked the next moment. Sigolene was gasping, "You look beautiful you know. Why do you have such blue eyes? It's scarce here."

"I don't know. Maybe because I don't belong here. I come from Kerman," and after a while she continued, "Could you continue caressing me? I should be ashamed of behaving like a little child, but I need it. It calms me."

Sigolene gave the woman a close hug and gently cuddled her hair and back. Their faces were so close at one moment. Sigolene was excited, "Forgive me this is maybe not the right moment and place to ask. I don't even know if you like to kiss a woman. I know Sahra forces you into it. But I so much love to kiss you. Could I maybe?"

Manda didn't say anything. She closed her eyes and opened them again a narrow slit. She nodded. Sigolene's heart beat fast. She brought her lips closer to Manda's. She kissed her, and then did it again. This time she didn't let Manda's lips go away. She necked with her affectionately.

∞ ∞ ∞

Sigolene was looking at Manda's sleeping face. Manda was cold out. Sigolene's feelings were rent between remorse and lust. Had she exploited Manda's hapless situation to kiss her? Had she asked of kissing her too soon? Would Manda have kissed her having not chained to a bed alone in a dungeon for three weeks? On the other hand Sigolene had so much lascivious thoughts: She wanted to go down on this woman and ask for the same. She wanted to melt into her. "Oh Manda, how beautiful you are, even with closed eyes!" She didn't know her mind entertained exactly the same thoughts Sahra once had.

She then looked at the small window beside the ceiling Manda had told her about. Was it the only means to escape this cellar? She'd been to other rooms with the flickering candle to search for a club or stick to fight Sahra when she came back. She hadn't found anything useful. But maybe next day she could climb up the bed's headboard and reflect the sunlight with the small compact she had brought along by chance in her gown's pocket, to signal someone, maybe even Mehran, to come to their help. She knew Mehran brought the horses every day to the stream to drink water. But she didn't know exactly when. How could she remain up there one entire day on the tip of the headboard to await someone to appear? She slowly fell asleep, her mind muddled by so many thoughts.

∞ ∞ ∞

Mehran hadn't seen Sigolene for two days now. When he had asked Soraya about her whereabouts, she'd said, "Sahra should know. I saw that arrogant French snob chasing that Persian fellow snob to out back the night before last night. I was watching them through the window. And that was the last time."

"Yes, but where to?"

"I don't know. I asked Sahra if she knew. I told her she was following her."

"You told her? Are you stupid?!"

"Why not? Or there is something I don't know. Tell me, I'd like to know."

"You said yourself the other day something strange was going on between Sahra and Manda. That you doubted if Sahra didn't know anything about Manda's disappearance."

"Yes, I doubted. However, what's it to you? I never liked that strange girl from Kerman. If Sahra has done anything to her, she has deserved it."

"Why?"

"Because she never listened to me. I wanted to be her friend but she spurned me. And now you come all wound up and worried about the whereabouts of your new French woman. Why no one is interested in me? Am I not fair enough and my eyes not light enough?"

Mehran took his leave as he saw the discussion would end nowhere. He went around the mansion for a walk. At one point, behind the mansion, the stairs down to the basement beside the cistern and its odd and frightening huge iron door caught his attention. He climbed down the stairs to look at it up close. It had patterns on it resembling a battlefield. Elephants whose riders were armed with spears on the one side confronting troops of javelin wielding masked warriors riding camels on the other. He pulled at the door. It scraped but didn't open. It was locked. He turned around and went up the stairs again. He headed for the Jome Mosque. The sheriff's office would be nearby.

∞ ∞ ∞

He entered the office as he heard flies buzzing around. The sheriff sat at his desk eating yogurt with dry flatbread. A huge picture of King Reza Shah in a simple khaki military uniform hung on the wall behind him. Under it he could read a script, "King of Kings, Reza Shah the Great is the guardian of our land, Persia."

"Come in," the sheriff called out to Mehran, "The assistant said you wanted to report someone missing."

"Yes, sir," Mehran like any other simple vassal was afraid at the sight of a man of law.

"Come here, sit here son," the sheriff pointed to a rickety metal stool in front of his desk. Mehran walked toward it slowly and took the seat.

The sheriff stroked his long mustache which punctuated his icy stare. "Now begin. I will continue with eating and you will talk, all right?"

After a while Mehran talked, "Sheriff I want to report that Madam Lofateau is missing."

"Madam who? You mean that French woman in the mansion of Mr. and Mrs. Malard?"

"Yes"

"No wonder she didn't appear yesterday at the station to explain her tasks. So this bitch has really done something wrong that she has vanished altogether to avoid the meeting."

The sheriff's tone and words annoyed Mehran and his features twitched. The sheriff took notice, "Do I see a note of brooding for that European woman?"

"I don't want to discuss if Lady Lofateau is doing a good job. I am here because in Mr. Malard's mansion, only around three weeks ago another woman went missing and I find it very suspicious that now Miss Lofateau has also disappeared."

"But the owner of the mansion, Mrs. Malard, says that servant went back to Kerman where she comes from."

"That's what she says. Actually I think she might be responsible herself. Everyone says she had issues with Manda, the missing woman."

"And she did have issues with your French girlfriend too?"

Mehran was surprised at the sheriff's wording but remained calm, "I don't know. Miss Lofateau told me she didn't like Mrs. Malard. Anyway today I was walking around the mansion and I found that the large iron door to the basement was locked. I swear that's new. I have been working for one year for the family and it was always open. I find it very fishy."

"I see you have made quite good friends with your European woman. Why fishy now? Because Mrs. Malard wants to avoid being robbed by burglars? I find your reasoning ridiculous."

"I swear I have a very bad feeling about this. Please do something! It doesn't take much. Just come over and ask Mrs. Malard to open the door."

"Do you only have a bad feeling or have you also heard something, like someone asking for help?"

"The basement is beside the cistern with openings into which the wind constantly blows. It sounds like a constant whimpering. It is very difficult to make out additional sounds if there."

"So you accuse a prominent family of this town on absurd grounds that you have a bad feeling or you miss your lover so much?"

"No..."

The sheriff cut in and didn't let Mehran go on, "Listen son! I don't see any reason why you should put your oar into police affairs. If I hear that you have broken into that cellar, I swear I will make the judge give you jail for several years. And now a piece of advice, don't take pity on that madam of yours. She looks at you, at us, as wild people. For her you are an uncivilized brute, almost an animal. Mind your own business."

Mehran was trembling out of rage, "So you won't do anything?"

"No"

CHAPTER FIFTEEN: TIME TO SAY GOODBYE

Sahra raised her lash similar to an Arab warrior brandishing a sword. Sigolene and Manda hugged each other in fear. "Now I have two women slaves! What can be any better? Two to pleasure me instead of one."

"You are crazy Sahra. You think you can get away with this? Sooner or later they will find us. I had an appointment with the sheriff today. Soon he will get suspicious and start looking for me," Sigolene was loud but a frisson of fright shot through her.

"Huh," Sahra laughed, "that policeman won't undertake anything without our permission. We are aristocrats, with ties to Qajars, for your information."

"Please Sahra. Be rational. Set us free! We won't say a word," Manda's voice wobbled.

"Oh my princess, my love! Don't fool around! I told you, I am more than happy to see Sigolene has joined you. Two women, two times the pleasure. One of you will suck my nipples, the other will eat me out. Group work, you know."

Sahra left moments later while Manda and Sigolene both shook.

"I am so thirsty," Sigolene looked at the small glass of water Sahra had brought along for them to drink.

"Go on, drink it all," Manda said softly loosening her grip on Sigolene's body so that she could reach for the glass of water.

"What about you?"

"I am not thirsty, go on!"

"I haven't seen you drink since yesterday."

Manda didn't answer. She just smiled and gave the cascade of blond hair running down Sigolene's shoulder a gentle stroke. Having drunk the water, Sigolene held Manda again tightly in her arms.

"I am so happy that you are here Sigolene."

Sigolene caressed Manda. She could feel Manda's heartbeat on her own bosom. It was the only thing that still soothed her in that afflicting circumstance. Moments after, she felt so much connection to the oriental woman in her arms, "I fell in love with your beauty the very first time I saw you. I wanted to ask you if I could shoot photos of you but I didn't dare. You would be a great picture on the first page of our newspaper back in Paris. I would give you a bunch of roses and dub the picture 'Persian woman, Persian roses.'"

"I wish I were not beautiful!"

"Why?"

"Maybe then Sahra wouldn't have fallen in love with me, and men wouldn't leer at me all the time. I envy Soraya, she's ugly but has a comfortable life."

"Does it bother you that I like you too?"

Manda looked Sigolene in her eyes. Her look was so piercing Sigolene got goosebumps. "May I share a secret with you?"

"Yes"

"I actually enjoy going down on Sahra, although I don't love her. I hate her, but when it comes to giving her head, I am happy."

Sigolene couldn't believe, "That's crazy! How can you hate her but enjoy doing that for her?"

"I don't know. Maybe it's because she is just such a miserable woman and I take pity on her, and want to make her happy. Her moaning touches my heart. It's the only moment when she sounds blissful. But every time I hate myself for having enjoyed it. I think Sahra knows that I like it. She is the receiver. And that's why she doesn't let go."

"Why do you tell me this? I didn't like it. You don't have to disclose all your secrets to others."

"Because I like you Sigolene. Unlike Sahra, I do. I am sure Sahra will set us free soon, and soon after you will go back to France, and we will never see each other again. So if you like I can go down on you right now."

"You mean it?" Sigolene gasped as she couldn't believe what she'd just heard. Was this woman acting again out of despair and tribulation? Her blank look seemed like that of a confused woman after all. So would it be abusive if she would receive oral sex from her? She wasn't sure, but her desire got the better of her.

Moments later, she shook as she watched those sea-blue eyes watch her from between her own thighs as she hyperventilated. "I love it Manda! Do it just like that!..."

∞ ∞ ∞

Sahra was all worked up that night. She was afraid. It was going to look very weird for sure. Two women having disappeared in the mansion in the same month? Would anyone try to enter the basement anytime soon? Should she try to find another hiding place for them? And was there only one key to the basement, or did Koorosh or someone else have another one? Was there anything in the basement which he would in the near future search? These and a lot of other questions passed her mind. Then again, she was excited. Could she really keep both those women in the basement in chains forever, and as she had put it herself, each pleasuring her in her own unique way? One lapping her privates and the other sucking her nipples, or kissing her foot? She needed that so much, that feeling of being adored and pampered by others. Those thoughts were so pleasing. She shook as she masturbated. She did it again, and again.

∞ ∞ ∞

The two light-eyed women were asleep, huddling as the metal door scraped again, making them jump in their skin. How much they hated this sound. They knew Sahra was up to no good showing up that time in the night. They braced themselves for the worst to come: Maybe two people entertaining that evil woman at the same time? The idea loathed Sigolene. She pressed herself hard against Manda's body.

"What the...?! What are you doing here?" Koorosh had appeared to search for the box of diamonds he'd hidden two years ago behind the mirror and couldn't believe the scene he saw: Two half-naked women chained to the bed in the last room of the basement!

∞ ∞ ∞

It hadn't taken long. As soon as Koorosh had heard the fragmented version of the story from the two women, he had seen his own chance. Now he could divorce Sahra without paying Mahriyeh, a large sum of money due in Persian culture if a man would divorce his wife. After freeing both women from chain, he had gone straight up to the unlucky Sahra to send her back to her parents' house. "You are so inhumane; a witch you are! I would burn you down right away hadn't the law bound my hands!"

"Go on, burn me down! Because then you will set me free. From the time my parents made me marry you and enter this dreary mansion of yours, it was as though I set foot on hell itself!"

"Get out of my sight!" Koorosh yelled. Sahra had only a duffle of items to transport as all her belongings actually had been her husband's he claimed. He was going to go to the sheriff and spill everything the very next day.

∞ ∞ ∞

"She is not an evil woman, it's unfair. They should put Koorosh in jail. He always treated her meanly." Manda lay in bed as Omme Salameh stirred the bowl of soup she had brought for her. Manda looked feeble. Around her eyes was red and bruised. Omme Salameh couldn't stand what she heard, "My child you are so selfless. Often as not I

110

admire your patience with others but now it angers me that you feel sorry for a woman who abused you so horribly. You should grow up my child. You know better than anyone else how she treated me, and I will never forgive her in my heart. Forgiving people is a fine deed and the way of saints. Then again all of us have the right not to excuse the people who wronged us."

Manda moaned in pain. Her wrists and ankles had been injured by the chain. Her look was pale and her face wan. Omme Salameh brought the bowl closer to her mouth and fed the Persian beauty with the spoon in her old wrinkled but kind hand. Manda ate the soup as she watched sparrows chirping on the willow tree through the window. For a moment, all the agony she'd experienced hitherto seemed to lie far past.

∞ ∞ ∞

Sigolene was in a hurry. She'd packed her clothes in her large ragged suitcase and her camera, tripod and paraphernalia in her carryall. Mustafa was waiting in the Tin Lizzie in front of the mansion. She wanted to run away from everything. From that ominous mansion with all that had happened there. From the sheriff who, after all the nightmare she'd been through, had asked her again to go to his office for the scrutiny of the photographs she'd made. "You should be honest about your photos of camels or women in chador. We want to show the world a progressive image of Persia," he had pushed again.

She tugged her gathered material out the room and across the courtyard. It was not easy, but she didn't want to ask anyone for help. She wanted only to vanish.

"You're leaving?!"

Startled, she turned around while she still had a grip on the suitcase and the large bag. It was Mehran. He was holding a bunch of fresh roses he had plucked from a garden in his own village. Sigolene's heart fell.

"Yes, I am. I am sorry I didn't let you know. I thought it would be better for both of us."

"The sheriff was right. For you I am a brute, an animal. As soon as I heard the story I gathered these flowers and hurried over to see how you are doing, and if you need anything, but now I see you are leaving without saying goodbye."

"Don't say that. Our friendship means a lot to me."

"Friendship? You call it only friendship? What about calling it love? Do friends make love? Does it count only as friendship?"

"Shush! Don't talk so loud," Sigolene was more embarrassed than ashamed. "I am so sorry I am doing this. But you should know that I like you too..."

"I love you!" Mehran cut in, "Take me with you Sigolene! I will do anything you need. I will clean your house, wash your dishes, I will cook."

Sigolene smiled and put her palm on Mehran's cheek. She felt his fast pulse under her skin. "I would have loved to taste the Persian dishes you cook. I can't take you with me, believe me Mehran, I can't. If I could I would, but I can't. You don't have the necessary documents. You don't know a single word French, and you need money. I can't afford to support you. I am on a tight budget."

No answer came. Mehran was trembling. Tears had welled up in his dark eyes. Sigolene took the small bouquet from him. "Thanks so much!" She sniffed at the roses, "They are so beautiful, and sweet-smelling!" Mehran was silent as tears ran down his face. "Miss Lofateau, we don't have all day!" Mustafa, the chauffeur, called out to Sigolene from the other side of the courtyard's gate.

"I will help you." Mehran took the suitcase and the bag and carried them to the car. He stood by as Mustafa popped up the trunk for the suitcase and carryall and opened the rear door for the French woman to sit. "I will write you," Sigolene said.

"We should hurry, they say there's going to be a storm in the afternoon." Mustafa said flatting the gas. Sigolene watched how Mehran and the mansion got smaller, and then the minarets of the Jome Mosque,

112

until they all vanished in the dazzling rays of the bright sun. Another chapter in her journalist career closed, at the heart of Persia.

∞ ∞ ∞

Koorosh opened the steel chest he'd brought from the basement. He was looking for the costly diamonds he had imported several years ago from India. One of them, actually the smallest one would be the gift he was going to present to Mrs. McKenzie. The lock was so old that the key couldn't turn. Should he oil the hole? He didn't have any at hand. He tried several times but the chest didn't unlock. He put the key aside and sighed angrily. Of a sudden, he thought of Mrs. McKenzie's shapely bare legs. Would she someday let him take off those panties of her? His heart beat fast as he finally decided to try yet another time, this time doing it slowly and with patience. The lock opened at the first try! He jerked the door open. He was dumbfounded! Inside there was nothing but a piece of paper. His eyeballs bulged out of their sockets as he read,

"Dear Koorosh. You don't believe but I have seen this day coming, somehow. Maybe the angels have talked to me when asleep or demons made me have the vision. However, I am sure when you are reading this letter you have divorced me and I am not in the mansion and out of your reach. So I dare give vent to my feelings and all the hate that has piled up in my heart. You never treated me fairly Koorosh! The very first day I came to your house my heart was full of hope. I was set to build a life with a good-looking man I thought was going to save me from the stringent atmosphere of my parents' home and treat me with the due respect I deserved as an educated woman. It didn't last long until the hearth of our small family turned cold and the warmth I felt being beside you at the beginning faded away. Soon life turned into a new hell for me, which was still harder for me to hold out than that of at my parents. The difference was that this time I didn't have any hope for improvement, there was going to be no future, and I was grown-up. Days and nights passed, years passed and I was ensnared in this mansion of yours which I called home on the outside, but considered my prison. How hurtful can life be if you are alone and have no one to turn to for help. My heart is but not only brimful with sadness, but also with rage. Now the only thing to which I can resort to alleviate my pain and my smarting heart is vengeance. I saw you looking at this diamond

113

you brought along from your trip to Delhi with admiring eyes. I beheld a look I had never known. I am sure at the time you are reading this note you have had affairs with numberless women, but I have never seen them. But this time I saw the look with which you would eye those women. That filled me with so much anger that I knew right away that it was my chance for revenge. I spied on you as to where you hid this box of diamonds which you said cost a fortune, and I knew where you were going to hide the key. Now dear Koorosh, your diamonds are out somewhere. They're among the dunes out back of the mansion. I have made sure you won't find them, but maybe you could give it a try. Good luck!"

"This wretch!" Koorosh trembled as he looked at the piece of paper in disbelief. He looked uncanny. He stood up. He looked out the window. It was high noon. The sun was shining with a searing heat. As though under a spell, he got out of the room to head towards the dunes behind the mansion. He watched the sea of hills on the other side of the stream stretching hundreds of miles to the mountains seen on the horizon. He stepped into the stream without taking off his shoes and waddled in the water. He was out of his mind. "This bitch! Where are my diamonds?" He looked at the rolling skyline. Could they be somewhere around? A handful of shiny pebbles lying on a hillfoot caught his attention. He ran to them to see up close. They were but only a pile of normal shiny sand. He straightened his back in anguish groaning, "Where are they? Oh God! Where are they?!" He addressed God Almighty as if he was just another servant of his. He ran to the next hill, and the next. The bright sun made much of the sand around look like dazzling diamonds.

Soon enough he was lost among the see of sand hills which all looked alike, and couldn't say where the mansion or the town was, but instead of trying to find the way back he kept searching for his diamonds for hours.

∞ ∞ ∞

No one saw Koorosh ever come back from the desert. He probably breathed his last still burning in greed and fantasy. If his last thoughts

were of his own diamonds or of Mrs. McKenzie's underwear, no one
would ever know.

THE END

Lightning Source UK Ltd.
Milton Keynes UK
UKHW020834270223
417728UK00016B/1347

9 798702 409177